Patrick Dolcet is hired by a friend of an ex-boyfriend to represent him when he enters a custody battle. While stopping at the client's place for a consultation, he comes across a man who pushes every last one of his buttons. Brand Erdogan is big, brawny, and has a friendly smile. Patrick isn't certain if the attraction is mutual, and Brand seems reluctant to start anything . . . for a few reasons. The man doesn't consider himself gay, or even bisexual. On top of that, Brand thinks Patrick — a successful custody lawyer — is way out of his league. With a little help from a friend, Brand agrees to join Patrick for dinner . . . and then another. Even though their actions are discrete, someone has it in for Patrick. When pictures of Patrick and Brand in a compromising position threaten not only his job, but his relationship with Brand, Patrick has to rely on the trust they've built. Will the chance at love be enough to keep Brand at Patrick's side? Or will one too many obstacles tear their possible future apart?

Pack Strap Carry
Copyright © 2019 Charlie Richards
ISBN: 978-1-4874-2590-6
Cover art by Angela Waters

Published by eXtasy Books Inc or
Devine Destinies, an imprint of eXtasy Books Inc

Look for us online at:
www.eXtasybooks.com or www.devinedestinies.com

PACK STRAP CARRY
CARRY ME: BOOK NINE

BY

CHARLIE RICHARDS

DEDICATION

Do not go where the path may lead, go instead where there is no path and leave a trail.
~Ralph Waldo Emerson

CHAPTER ONE

Patrick Dolcet kept the smile pasted on his face even though he would much rather have glared at his belligerent date. This was the last time he would agree to a blind date from one of the partners at his firm. One way or another, Patrick would find a way out of it.

Maybe that's what I'll do when I get home . . . think up a list of acceptable excuses.

"So, I was thinking we could skip dessert," Walter stated. Resting his forearms on the table, he leaned toward Patrick and leered at him. "I'd much rather we head to my hotel room and fuck." Walter hummed as he perused Patrick's body — what he could see of it anyway. "I want to sink my dick in your tight ass so damn bad. You ready to go?"

Good grief. The nerve of this guy!

So shocked, Patrick had to clear his throat before finding his voice. "Uh, as flattering as that is, I'm sorry, Walter. I have a meeting with a client tomorrow morning, and there's still a few things I need to get together." He did his best to keep his tone even, not allowing the disgust he felt to bleed through.

Walter snorted as he shook his head. "I don't want to sleep with you. I just want to fuck you." He lifted his hand, obviously attempting to get the waitress's attention. "There'll still be plenty of time for you to do that after I fill your ass."

The arrival of the waitress gave Patrick a second to think. "Hey, gentlemen. Can I interest you in some coffee or dessert?" she asked with a perky smile.

Gentlemen. Ha! If she only knew.

1

"No, thanks," Walter replied. "Just the check."

"Of course," she replied before turning away and heading off.

Walter stood, saying, "While you take care of that, I'm gonna go piss. Be right back."

Patrick watched in silence as Walter walked toward the back of the restaurant. As soon as his date was out of sight, relief flooded him. He pulled out his wallet.

As much as it galled Patrick to pay for Walter's dinner without a fight, it was just the break he needed. He slid a pen and the receipt from his cab ride to the restaurant from the inside of his suit coat pocket. On the back of the slip of paper, Patrick wrote a quick note.

I received an emergency call from a client. The dinner is paid for. Have a good night.

Patrick left the note on Walter's empty plate, then returned the pen to his pocket. Without waiting for the check, he pulled his wallet out. He had a good idea of how much the dinner had cost, so he left ample cash on the table.

Then Patrick swiftly exited the restaurant.

Crossing the sidewalk to the street, Patrick glanced up and down the road. He spotted a taxi in the distance and stuck out his arm to flag it down. To his relief, the taxi stopped, and he quickly climbed inside.

After giving the cabbie his address, Patrick relaxed back in the seat and heaved a grateful sigh.

"Long day, sir?" the cabbie asked, glancing at him in the rearview mirror.

Patrick focused on the man. "No," he replied with a shake of his head. "A bad date."

The cabbie's expression turned commiserating. "I remember those. Never been more grateful than when I found my wife." The man's smile became one of fondness. "Now I don't have to worry about that anymore."

Upon recognizing the look of adoration on the man's face

as he spoke of the woman who was obviously the love of his life, Patrick felt a pang of something in the vicinity of his heart. He wished someone would feel that way about him. Unfortunately, so far, all his attempts at relationships had failed miserably.

Thirty-one years old, and the longest relationship I've managed is four months.

That had been with a firefighter named Trace, and they'd ended amicably. The relationship had just sort of . . . fizzled. They were even still friends. In fact, Trace was the one who'd given his card to the client he had to see in the morning.

Once again, Patrick had to force a smile. "I'm happy for you."

The cabbie must have read something in his tone, for he gave him a reassuring smile. "You'll find her, son. Have faith."

Patrick couldn't remember the last time someone hadn't taken one look at him and jumped to the conclusion that he was gay. Hell, he not only wore lip gloss but eyeliner as well. Of course, it could have been because the cabbie was more focused on the road.

"*Him*," Patrick corrected softly. "And I sure hope so." This time, Patrick didn't have to force his smile. "It'd be really nice to have someone to come home to after a long day."

Without missing a beat, the cabbie replied, "Find *him*, then. If a relationship is what you want, never stop looking." He grinned as he used his rearview mirror to meet Patrick's gaze for an instant before returning his focus to the road. "There's a soul mate out there for everyone."

Nodding, Patrick prayed the man was right.

The trill of Patrick's phone caught his attention. He pulled it out and grimaced. Having no desire to talk to Walter, he denied the call, sending it to voicemail.

A moment later, his phone beeped, indicating Patrick had a message. Patrick pressed a button and lifted the phone to his ear. Walter's angry voice came through the line.

"You just think you're gonna cut and run on me, man? I was promised you'd put out. I can't wait to tell Freedman you made a liar out of him." Walter's voice lowered to a nasty snarl as he added, "I also think I'm gonna start a few rumors unless you're at my hotel in thirty minutes. Get your ass over here, or you'll be sorry."

Patrick was already sorry . . . sorry he'd allowed Richard Freedman to talk him into a date with Walter. While the man was a senior partner, Patrick should have known better. He should never have decided to do a little brown nosing.

When the cabbie came to a stop before Patrick's small home, he pulled out his wallet and gave the man a nice tip. He climbed out and headed up the walk. By the time he'd walked into his home, Patrick had decided on his course of action.

Leaving his keys on the hook by the door, Patrick headed to the kitchen. He grabbed a tumbler, then added a couple of ice cubes. When Patrick reached the sideboard, he filled his glass with spiced rum.

Patrick took a sip as he crossed to his sofa. The beverage caused his tongue to tingle, and his taste buds sang pleasantly. After swallowing the mouthful, Patrick set his tumbler on the coffee table so he could remove his jacket.

After draping his suit jacket over the back of the sofa, Patrick picked up the handset phone from the end table. It had been on his *to do* list forever to get rid of the landline, but he'd been too busy . . . or too lazy. There always seemed to be something more important than making a call to a phone center and dealing with a pushy sales representative.

Now it's a good thing.

Patrick dialed Richard's number. While he didn't consider the man a friend, not really, he'd collaborated with him on cases enough times that he felt comfortable ringing him at nine-thirty at night. As he waited for Richard to answer his call, Patrick picked up his drink and settled in his recliner.

"Hey, Patrick," Richard offered by way of greeting. "Everything going okay? Calling to thank me?"

As if.

"Hi, Richard." Patrick hesitated just a second, then told the other man, "Afraid not. Walter and I didn't hit it off. Not my type, but I was going to ask you how well you knew the man."

"Not exceptionally well," Richard admitted. "I met him at a conference three years ago. He hit on me, and I told him I wasn't gay." Chuckling softly, he admitted, "Flattering, but even if I was bisexual, he wouldn't be my type. I like my partners with some weight to them."

That was probably more than Patrick needed to know about Richard's sex life but whatever.

Before Patrick could respond, Richard asked, "Why do you ask?"

"Well, he made a number of inappropriate comments and expected me to let him fuck me," Patrick stated, deciding to be blunt. "When I attempted to politely decline, he pushed the issue, so I left. Then he left a message on my phone that could be taken as threatening."

For several long seconds, no sound came through the line. Patrick even pulled his phone away from his ear to be certain he hadn't dropped the call. The timer still ticked away.

Finally, his voice low and quiet, Richard stated, "He can definitely be an ass, but are you sure about being threatened? Could you have misunderstood?"

Patrick wasn't surprised that Richard didn't want to believe ill of his friend. "Well, take a listen to this, and tell me what you think." He was glad he'd saved Walter's message. As Patrick pulled it up on his cell phone, he commented, "You can tell me if it's all bluster."

The sound of Walter's voice filled the air, and Patrick hoped it would carry through the line. When the belligerent man finished speaking, silence fell again. Patrick waited . . .

impatiently.

Finally, Richard's deep sigh came through the line. "Yeah, that . . ." He sighed again. "I didn't tell him you'd have sex with him. I'd mentioned your name a few times over the years, and he wanted to meet you."

"Well, we met," Patrick replied dryly. He scoffed as he thought about his evening. "I just thought you should know how it turned out. That way if he calls —" Patrick paused, uncertain how to explain his aversion to the asshole without sounding like a judgmental ass himself.

"I get it," Richard murmured. "If he calls, I'll deal with it."

"I appreciate it," Patrick replied, a wave of relief washing over him. "Sorry to interrupt your night."

"No, it's fine. This'll teach me to never play matchmaker," Richard grumbled. "Not ever again."

Patrick laughed. He knew that feeling all too well. Realizing he didn't have anything else to say, Patrick cleared his throat. "Well, I think I'm gonna enjoy this rum, take a shower, and review some case files."

"Sounds like an exciting evening," Richard replied. "Good night."

"Night." Then Patrick disconnected the line and set both phones on the coffee table.

Patrick did exactly as he'd told the other man, and when he received another call from Walter, he silenced his phone and ignored the message.

I'll deal with it tomorrow.

Patrick followed the directions his GPS device issued, easily finding the pig farm owned by Laramie Goshen. While he'd never been there, he knew his ex-boyfriend, Trace, lived there, too. He wasn't visiting them though.

Instead of taking the main driveway to the ranch house, Patrick turned left onto a spur. He drove to one of two small cabins that had been built off to the side. Stopping in front of the larger of the pair, Patrick shifted his vehicle into park before cutting the engine.

As Patrick opened the door, he grabbed his satchel off the front seat. He climbed out and closed the door before peering up at the large cottage-style house. There was a good-sized front porch with a pair of rockers and an end table between them.

Patrick bet it was a nice place to pass a quiet evening.

Crossing to the cabin, Patrick realized he could just make out the scent of stain, telling him the porch had recently been redone. He paused at the bottom and reached out to touch the railing lightly. When his fingers encountered only dry wood, Patrick let out a relieved hum.

"Mark and I stained the deck over the weekend," a deep voice stated, drawing Patrick's attention upward. A black-haired, hazel-eyed man peered down at him with an amused smile curving his lips. "It's dry."

Patrick climbed the couple of stairs as he smiled back at the man. "Sorry about that. Just needed to check." Holding out his hand, Patrick introduced himself. "I'm Patrick Dolcet."

"Vance Weimer. Thanks for coming." Vance took Patrick's hand and shook, then released him and beckoned. "Please come in. Sorry I couldn't get to you at the office. I have a problem sow about ready to give birth, and I need to be here in case there's complications."

"I completely understand," Patrick replied, following Vance into the house. While the furniture appeared a bit old and well-worn, everything seemed clean. "I'm happy to come to you. It's good to get out of the office on occasion."

Vance led him to the sofa, and Patrick sat down, setting his briefcase beside his leg on the floor. After Vance had taken a seat in the nearby chair, he watched the man lean forward and rest his forearms on his legs. Vance heaved a sigh, and his brows furrowed.

"So, where should I begin?"

Patrick offered the obviously stressed man an encouraging smile. "How about at the beginning." He rested his palms on his thighs and waited.

Nodding, Vance straightened. "Okay. My ex-wife has majority custody of my son, Mark, and now that I'm in a relationship with a man, I'm certain she's going to try to keep him from me." Rubbing his fingers through his black hair, Vance continued, "I've also been funding her life for the last ten years after the divorce, and I'm tired of it. I want to fight for custody of my son, and I intend to force my ex to either get a job or she's gonna have to move, because I'm not paying for her giant house anymore, and I—" Vance growled as he rubbed his palm over his face.

The frustration pulsing from Vance was nearly a palpable thing, and Patrick's desire to help ease the man's ire rose. His need to help others was one of the reasons he'd become a lawyer specializing in child custody. He wanted to help families.

"Vance, your ex can't keep your son away from you just because you're in a homosexual relationship," Patrick told the clearly frazzled man. "You said she doesn't work, and you pay her way. Unless you're an abusive asshole, which I doubt because Trace recommended you"—he lifted his brows, pleased to see the stricken look on Vance's face as he quickly shook his head—"the law is on your side. Not hers."

CHAPTER TWO

Brand Erdogan strode swiftly out of the pig barn. As soon as he shut the door, cutting off the sound of squealing and grunting pigs, he paused for an instant to give his ears a chance to stop ringing. As much as he loved the sight of tiny, newly born piglets, getting through the birthing process always left his stomach unsettled.

Blowing out a harsh breath, Brand rubbed his hand over his belly. He swallowed once, twice, then inhaled through his nose before letting it out of his mouth. After doing that a second time, he felt his stomach begin to settle.

Deciding some food and maybe a drink would be a good idea, Brand started toward his cabin. Halfway across the yard, he groaned. His refrigerator was damn near empty.

Brand changed directions. He strode toward Vance's place instead. His buddy of over twelve years was a great cook and always had something fantastic in the refrigerator.

Vance baked in bulk a couple of times a week, so there were always leftovers.

Thinking about food, Brand felt the queasiness disappear — *thank god* — and his stomach began to rumble. Anticipation filled him. Picking up his pace, he grinned.

"Oh, huh," Brand muttered as he rounded the side of the large cabin and spotted the sedan parked in front of Vance's house. He scowled. "That's not Jimmy's car."

Brand knew Vance's lover, Jimmy Gibson, only lived with Vance half the time. His friend was trying to get Jimmy to move in permanently, but he hadn't had luck quite yet. Jimmy seemed to want to make certain everything worked out with the custody battle Vance was about to enter with his ex-wife before he moved in permanently.

As Brand's booted feet clomped across the wooden porch planks, he heard voices coming through the open window and closed screen door.

"I've already talked to my son about living here more often," Vance was telling someone. "He was surprised, to say the least." He growled in irritation before continuing, "I guess Darlene's been filling his head with comments about how I'm so busy and don't bother making any extra time to spend with him. Mark plays baseball, and I didn't even know. The damn bitch ordered Mark not to tell me."

Peering through the screen door, Brand watched Vance scrub his hands through his short, black hair, a sure sign of his frustration. His own ire spiked upon processing his buddy's words. Brand knew for a fact that Vance would have been to every game if he'd known.

Brand pulled open the screen door, and his focus shifted to the man sitting on the sofa who had his back toward him. The faint squeak of the door caused Vance to peer over the stranger's head. Then the other man turned, and Brand found himself peering into the deepest gray eyes he'd ever seen . . . even through the black-rimmed spectacles he wore.

"Mark plays baseball?" Brand towed off his boots before heading across the room toward the kitchen, nearly stumbling before he managed to yank his gaze away from the stranger's beautiful eyes so he could watch where he was going. "When's his next game?"

Damn. Beautiful eyes? Did I just think that?

"His new season starts in a week," Vance replied. "What are you doing here?"

"Sow eighty-seven birthed fifteen piglets. Six males and nine females," Brand told him as he grabbed a mug and the coffee carafe, returning his focus to why he was there. "And I came for food. Whadaya got in the fridge?"

Vance snorted, his tension easing as his shoulders relaxed. "Chicken enchiladas. Help yourself."

"Nice! Yum!" As Brand took a sip of his drink, his attention once more strayed to the stranger. The man's lips gleamed in the light, and he realized the guy wore lip gloss. When Brand's gaze slid back to the man's gray eyes, he spotted the heated admiration in them . . . as well as the eyeliner that accentuated the irises. "You want some?"

Brand fought back the heat that threatened to slide up his neck to his face.

Shit! When was the last time I blushed?

And why did I ask him to join me for food?

"That sounds like a good idea," Vance stated, rising from his chair. Even though Brand spotted the questioning tilt of his buddy's brow, he still beckoned to his guest while saying, "This is my best friend, Brand Erdogan. He's aware of everything I'm telling you, so please know you can speak freely." As the man rose and followed Vance toward the dining room table, Vance continued, "Brand, this is Patrick Dolcet. He's the custody lawyer who's gonna help me out of this mess with Darlene."

The way the lean man—even discernable in his expensive-looking suit—moved across the room made him appear to glide. His hips swayed in an oddly enticing way. Brand even thought his five-foot-nine frame put him at the perfect height—not too tall to tuck against Brand's own six-foot-five frame, but not too short, either.

Good grief! I must need to get laid if I'm thinkin' like this.

"Oh, yeah?" Brand put his coffee mug down and stepped closer, holding out his hand. This was his buddy's custody lawyer. *Not someone to trifle with and way out of my league.* "Glad to hear it. It's about damn time."

"Shut the fuck up," Vance growled.

Brand chuckled as he shook Patrick's hand. He felt the

hairs on the back of his arm stand on end upon feeling the soft flesh against his own more calloused palm. After releasing Patrick, he turned and headed back to the refrigerator. Before opening the door, he flipped Vance the bird.

To Brand's surprise, he heard a soft chuckle from behind him. He grabbed the large baking dish, which was still over halfway full of chicken enchiladas. Glancing over his shoulder, Brand spotted the smirk curving Patrick's lips. Not only was there a sparkle in the man's eyes, but he noticed that Vance's guest had been staring at his ass.

Huh.

Brand pretended not to notice. While he'd accepted a blowjob from a guy a few times, he didn't consider himself gay . . . or even bisexual. Hell, his dick didn't know the difference between a man's mouth or a woman's.

What would this guy's mouth feel like on my dick?

Damn. Definitely been too long.

Shutting down that line of thinking, Brand focused on the food. He placed the dish on the counter, then opened the cupboard to his left. After grabbing three plates and setting them on the counter, too, he pulled a spatula from a canister, then began serving a couple of enchiladas on each plate.

"Uh, are you the boyfriend, then?" Patrick asked from where he leaned against the table.

As Brand barked a laugh and shook his head, Vance stated, "No. Most definitely not."

"Aww . . . what?" Brand teased while putting the first plate into the microwave. Turning back to face his friend, he waggled his brows. "Am I not your type, hot stuff?"

Vance rolled his eyes. "You know that you're not." He grabbed a couple more mugs and held one up. "Want some coffee, Patrick? Or water, beer, wine." Pointing at the sideboard, Vance added, "Or maybe something stronger so you can tolerate Brand's poor attempts at humor?"

Brand heard the microwave beep so focused on switching

out the food. "You just hate that I'm funnier than you."

"Yeah, that's it," Vance responded, his tone dry. "And my boyfriend is named Jimmy. Jimmy Gibson."

"Jimmy Gibson?" Patrick repeated, recognition filling his words. "The bartender at The Red Door?"

After starting the microwave again, Brand glanced over his shoulder just in time to see Vance's huge grin. "Yep. That's my man," Vance claimed, clearly pleased with himself.

For an instant, Brand actually felt a pang of . . . something. Jealousy, he realized, much to his chagrin. He felt no attraction to either man, but there was a small part of him that wanted what Vance and Jimmy had found together.

Damn. When did I start feeling like this?

While Brand shoved the last plate into the microwave to heat, he tried to figure out the answer to that question. The sensation had to have been creeping up on him for a while — maybe even years before when he'd watched Laramie and Trace fall for each other.

When Brand began placing the dishes onto the table, he realized he'd missed part of the conversation. Vance and Patrick had already sat down at the table. Both men had cups of coffee cradled between their palms, and Patrick was outlining the paperwork needed for Vance to move forward with his plans.

"Thank you, Brand," Vance murmured as he leaned back and accepted the plate. Then his hazel eyes twinkled with mischief as he stated, "You're gonna make someone a fine wife someday."

Brand growled, glaring at him. "Funny." Gripping the edge of Vance's plate, he began to pull it away from him. "I'll just put this back."

Vance grabbed his fork and whapped the back of it against Brand's knuckles. "Hands off," he ordered.

"Ow, damn it," Brand grumbled, releasing the plate. "Ass."

"Thief," Vance immediately countered.

"Jerk," Brand quipped back.

Vance smirked. "Mooch."

Brand narrowed his eyes. "Pussy-whipped."

Laughing, Vance shook his head. "Dick-whipped."

Barking a laugh of his own, Brand lifted his hands in sur-render. "You win."

Vance grinned back at him. "Yep."

Brand grabbed his own coffee and settled at the table with the others. Picking up his fork, Brand glanced between the men—doing his best not to allow his focus to linger on Patrick. He scooped up a healthy forkful and shoved it into his mouth.

Groaning softly, Brand relished the creamy, cheesy flavor bursting over his tongue. As soon as he swallowed, he ate another bite. He chewed and swallowed that one just as fast.

As Brand ate that bite, he realized the other men were staring at him. After he'd swallowed, he glanced between them. Vance's lips were curved in amusement, and Patrick stared at him with a wide-eyed look.

"What?" Brand lifted a napkin to his mouth. "I got something on my face?"

Vance chuckled as he shook his head. "No. Just always entertaining to see how much you love eating my food."

Brand pointed his fork at the chicken enchiladas. "Can you blame me? This crap is amazing!" He slid his fork into his enchilada again. "I can't cook for shit, so . . . mmm," he hummed as he took another bite.

"You like Italian?" Patrick asked as he slid the tines of his fork into his own food.

Glancing Patrick's way, Vance dipped his chin in a nod. "Yeah, love it," he replied after he'd swallowed his bite of food. "Why?"

Patrick narrowed his eyes a little, and he held Brand's gaze. "I make an amazing chicken parmesan. You want to try it?"

Brand sucked down his surprised gasp as he took in the hungry gleam in Patrick's gray eyes. The move also caused a piece of food to go down his throat the wrong way. Choking roughly, he pounded the fist of his free hand on his chest as his eyes watered.

After a few seconds, Brand managed to draw in a rough breath. He coughed it right back out again. Grabbing his coffee mug, he carefully took a sip, then another.

"Wow, I didn't realize offering to make dinner for a hot guy would cause such alarm," Patrick commented in a mild tone. He swept his gaze up and down Brand's body a couple of times before adding, "Surely you get asked out all the time, Brand."

Brand began slowly shaking his head as he continued to try to get his breath. Not trusting himself to speak, he could only stare wide-eyed at the man. Seeing the way Patrick arched his slender eyebrow in disbelief, Brand opened his mouth, then shut it again.

This handsome lawyer just asked me out on a date? Why the hell would he do that?

"I think what Brand is struggling with is two-fold. First, you're going to be my lawyer, and Brand is a friend . . . so being asked out in my home is probably damn unexpected."

Vance began to easily voice Brand's thoughts, which he appreciated, since he was still catching his breath by drinking small sips of coffee.

"I admit I probably shouldn't have, seeing as I'm still conversing with you about what we need to go ahead with filing a request to change your custody agreement," Patrick began slowly, his cheeks taking on a slight pinkish hue. His gray eyes had darkened to a stormy color, betraying either his discomfort or his desire. "But you're hot, and I like the way you were looking at me when I walked into the dining room. I want to find out if our chemistry is anything we can build on."

Oh, holy fucking shit. Is this guy for real? What the hell could a handsome and probably rich lawyer want with a working grunt like me?

"And that brings me to my second point," Vance stated softly. His left brow lifted as he glanced between them, and his concern was evident to Brand. "I'm not certain Brand swings your way, regardless of how you think he's been looking at you." Vance's brows furrowed, and he took on a confused expression. "Unless . . . there's something you want to share?"

Brand finally felt as if he'd caught his breath. "You wanna make me dinner because you want me to fuck you?" He couldn't help the rasp of his tone, and he sure hoped the table hid the bulge behind his fly that betrayed the thickening of his dick.

I am not entertaining this idea.

Patrick immediately shook his head even as his cheeks darkened further. "I said I think you're hot, and I like the way you look at me," he corrected softly. After a shrug of his shoulders, he added, "I like sex, sure, but I don't want to jump right into bed with you. No matter how hot you are. I want to get to know you." His focus shifted to Vance. "Since you're buddies and living on Trace and Laramie's pig farm, can I assume that Laramie doesn't have abusive assholes working for him?"

Brand saw the hint of fear that crossed Patrick's face before the man once again cleared his features. A surge of anger rushed through him. "Someone hurt you," he growled. He hated bullies . . . hated people who used their strength against another. "Who the fuck was it? I'll teach 'em." Brand even cracked his knuckles, eager to give the beat-down.

As a big man — six-foot-five with plenty of muscles — Brand didn't get challenged often. That didn't mean he didn't know how to handle himself, though. He'd been in a few bar fights and had gotten himself into plenty of scrapes as a teenager.

Patrick chuckled as he shook his head. "I'm not going to

answer that."

"You know what," Vance cut in. "If you can do dessert, I bet Brand will say yes."

Brand gaped, his ire disappearing almost instantly as he snapped his gaze to his buddy. "What?"

What the hell is Vance doing?

Vance winked at him. "Go on, man. Have a free meal, and get to know Patrick." He reached across the table and smacked Brand on his upper arm. "What could it hurt?"

Even as Brand opened his mouth, intending to say *it could hurt plenty*, Patrick stated, "No Italian meal is complete without tiramisu for dessert."

Brand inhaled deeply. Even as the delicious aroma of the chicken enchiladas flooded his nostrils, his mouth watered for a whole new reason. He swallowed and licked his lips.

God, I am so ruled by my stomach.

"When?" Brand asked. "Where?"

CHAPTER THREE

"I have no idea what I was thinking," Patrick mumbled into the phone.

Gary laughed. "That's because you were thinking with your dick."

Patrick groaned, dropping his head back onto the sofa's cushion. "I *know*! The words just came out . . . me . . . asking Brand to dinner." Remembering that moment, he felt his cheeks heat anew. "Just . . . the sounds he was making while eating the chicken enchiladas made my dick so hard it hurt. I couldn't even stand up when he said goodbye and left, or I would have shown off a raging erection." Thinking back on that, the arousal that had begun to rise in him quickly diminished. "Brand wasn't going to accept," Patrick admitted. "And his buddy says he doesn't think Brand swings my way."

"Doesn't *think* . . ." Now Gary sounded confused. "Wouldn't Brand have just said something? You were all sitting together, right?"

"Well, yeah, but—" Patrick couldn't quite make himself admit that he hadn't been confident enough to ask outright. "The conversation moved back to what I was supposed to be there for anyway. Then ten minutes later, Brand left."

"So . . . you have a handsome, sexy man that pushes all your buttons and makes your dick hard coming to dinner tonight, and you don't know if he's interested in you . . . *like that* . . . or even could be?"

"Right."

Gary sighed. "Wow, Pat. This impulsiveness isn't like you."

"I *know*." Patrick lifted his head only to allow it to flop back onto the cushion. "Why would I do this to myself?"

Once again, Gary chuckled, but this time, the sound was full of light mirth. "Take a deep breath, Patrick," he encouraged. "This isn't the end of the world. He knows you're attracted to him, right?"

"Yes." Patrick had been straightforward with the man, at least.

"And he still agreed. That means there's at least a possibility."

Patrick so wanted to agree . . . but he knew better. "Brand agreed for the food," he admitted.

"Then feed the man and be his friend." Gary snickered. "You know what they say" — his tone turned suggestive — "the way to a man's heart is through his stomach."

Snorting, Patrick nodded absently, even though he knew Gary couldn't see it. "Yeah." He knew it was the best advice. "I'll feed him and see where it goes."

Patrick's biggest fear was that it wouldn't go anywhere, but he couldn't figure out why. He'd met the man for less than thirty minutes at a client's home. Patrick didn't understand why he was already so invested in whether the guy liked him or not.

Maybe I'm just feeling a little raw from that date with Walter . . . and his continued annoying messages.

Walter had left three more messages over the following days. Each one was more descriptive than the last about what he intended to do to Patrick once they got together again. He was becoming damn stalker-ish.

The hairs on Patrick's arms stood up each time he thought about it. He'd saved the messages and prayed the calls would stop when Walter returned home. If that didn't happen, Patrick knew he would have to reach out to a couple of detective acquaintances.

"Patrick? You still there?"

Realizing he'd gotten lost in his head, Patrick returned his focus to Gary and his phone call. "Yeah, sorry about that. Just thinking."

"About Brand?" Gary teased suggestively.

Patrick groaned softly, then admitted, "Afraid not." He then went through the process of explaining Walter, his blind date, and the catastrophic aftermath.

Gary commiserated for a few minutes, then Patrick told him he had to run, or he wouldn't have enough time to make the food he'd promised.

"Call me later and tell me how it goes," Gary ordered.

"If I don't contact you tonight, then I'll call you tomorrow," Patrick promised. If the evening went poorly, he knew he wouldn't be in the mood to chat.

And if the night goes well, maybe I won't be alone so won't want to call in that case, either.

Patrick mentally groaned upon hearing his inner slut's thoughts.

"All right. Have a good night."

"Thanks." After Patrick said good night back, he disconnected the line, then forced himself back to his feet.

He placed his phone on the kitchen counter and began pulling out the supplies to make the tiramisu.

As the time for Brand's arrival approached, Patrick's nerves spiked. Even as he thrummed with anticipation at seeing the huge, handsome man again, he wondered if he should have learned a bit more about him before inviting him into his home. Patrick was so much smaller than Brand, after all.

While Patrick couldn't dismiss those thoughts entirely, he did manage to force them to the back of his mind. He would remain vigilant about not offending the man, but he intended to make his attraction known, too. That way, Patrick could confirm whether Brand just wanted to be friends or not.

That would suck, but from the way Brand and Vance interacted, I bet he'd make a great friend.

With the tiramisu in the refrigerator and the chicken parmesan in the oven, Patrick hurried to his bedroom. He changed into a nice pair of blue jeans, then went to the bathroom. After brushing his teeth, he styled his hair.

When Patrick lifted his eyeliner pencil, he paused.

What if Brand doesn't like make-up on a man?

Patrick growled under his breath, then applied the liner. If Brand didn't like it, then that was his problem. Besides, Patrick's momma had always told him never to change his looks, behavior, or personality for anyone.

A pang of sadness stabbed at Patrick's heart as he thought of his momma. Still, as he finished with the pencil, he smiled. His momma had been a wonderful, caring, and supportive woman.

While Patrick missed her dearly, he knew she was in a better place. Once his father had died in a construction accident—he'd been a framer—his mother had never found another to replace him. Patrick had been eight at the time, and he didn't have too many memories of the man, but his momma had told him wonderful stories about his robust and active father.

Maybe that's why I'm so attracted to big, strong men. Runs in the family.

Once, Patrick had asked why she didn't date—he'd been fourteen at the time and had just come out to her—and she'd told him she'd already found her one true love. No other man would ever be able to compare. Then she'd told him that when he met his own one and only, he would understand.

Patrick still waited for that day.

The sound of his doorbell ringing pulled Patrick out of his thoughts. He glanced at the alarm clock on his nightstand even as he hurried from the bathroom and through the bedroom. Noticing it was two minutes before the half-hour, Patrick smiled to himself.

Brand is punctual.

Patrick considered that a point in the man's favor. On instinct, he peered through the peek hole before opening the door. Spotting a broad chest encased in a red and blue flannel shirt, revealed by the open black jacket his guest wore, Patrick felt his heart rate spike.

With his heart threatening to pound right out of his chest, Patrick took a step back, unlocked the door, and gripped the knob. He took a quick, fortifying breath, then opened the door. Nearly swallowing his tongue upon viewing the sexy man standing on his porch, Patrick barely remembered to smile.

"Hi." Patrick swallowed hard, forcing moisture into his too-dry throat. He couldn't believe how breathy he sounded.

Brand's smile appeared just a little uncertain . . . or maybe that was the way his white hat cast a shadow over much of his face. "Hi."

Get your act together, Pat, or you're gonna scare him away before he even gets through the door.

While clearing his throat, Patrick took a step backward. "Thanks for coming." He beckoned with his fingers, then swept his arm to indicate the interior of his home. "Please, come on in."

Nodding once, Brand stepped forward. He glanced around as he hesitated in the foyer. "Should I take my boots off?" He asked, his focus on the carpeted floor of Patrick's home, which started five feet away.

Patrick looked at Brand's black boots. They appeared a little worn, but they were clean, and they were clearly dress boots. "No," he whispered absently as he swept his gaze up Brand's dark-jeans-covered calves to his thick thighs. Patrick felt arousal churning in his gut.

His gaze faltered at Brand's package.

Brand's front-bump promised something exquisite hidden behind his fly.

"So, *that's* how a woman feels when a man ogles her tits."

Upon hearing Brand's softly rumbled words, Patrick snapped his gaze to the man's face. He spotted the way his guest's lips were quirked into a half-smile. His dark eyes even appeared to twinkle.

"Uh, well . . . I'd say sorry, but I hate lying." Patrick rubbed the back of his neck as he did his best to return Brand's relaxed smile. "How about I say . . . I'll try not to openly stare and make you uncomfortable."

Brand lifted one wide shoulder in a half-shrug. "Naw, don't worry about it, man." He began moving his left arm from behind his back. "Makes me feel better about these."

Patrick hadn't even realized that Brand had kept one arm hidden. Then he spotted the bouquet of wildflowers. Glancing between the lovely array of blue, yellow, and pink flowers as well as Brand's eyes, Patrick found himself at a loss for words.

Shifting from foot to foot, Brand betrayed his discomfort. "Look. I know you're a guy," he began slowly. "But I don't date. Like . . . ever. It's probably been seven years, and that was a girl. I asked Vance, and he said it'd be okay, but if—"

Hearing Brand's rambling words caused Patrick's nerves to recede. It was replaced by giddiness.

Brand thinks this is a date! Yes!

"They're beautiful. Thank you." Getting his act together, he reached out and took them. He peered at Brand through his lashes as he lifted them to his nose and took a deep breath. "They smell wonderful. Never had anyone bring me flowers. I appreciate it." Patrick finally remembered Brand's earlier question and gave him a more thorough answer. "No, you don't have to take off your boots. But there's a coat rack to the left of the door if you want to get more comfortable."

Brand nodded and did as Patrick suggested, shrugging out of his jacket.

"I know I probably told you with my expression, but it bears saying out loud," Patrick stated, hoping to move them out of the awkward hello stage. "You look amazing."

"Thanks."

Brand not only placed the jacket on the free-standing coat stand Patrick kept beside the front door, but he also removed his white hat and hung it on a hook, too. Then he turned to face Patrick. Threading his fingers through his dark-brown hair, Brand was probably attempting to settle it into place, but the thick strands seemed to have a mind of their own.

Probably why he was wearing the hat.

While Brand let out a deep breath full of irritation, Patrick grinned. "Your hair is sexy, too." He waved his hand up and down, indicating Brand's entire form. "It suits you."

"Yeah?" Brand's lips curved back into the crooked grin that Patrick was really beginning to like.

Patrick nodded, offering an answering wide smile. "Oh, yeah."

Brand's grin broadened. "Thanks." Then he inhaled deeply, and he licked his lips. "Damn, Patrick. Something smells amazing in here."

Remembering how he'd convinced Brand to join him in the first place — by promising him delicious food — Patrick turned and headed down the hall. "The chicken should be done soon," he told his date. "Let me check the timer."

"Okay. Can I do anything to help?"

Patrick nodded. "Sure. I picked out a good merlot to go with our meal. It's in the fridge. Do you want to—" A thought occurred to Patrick as he opened a cupboard to get a vase to place the flowers in. "Oh." He turned to face Brand. "Do you like wine? I have a few beers from a local micro-brewery in my laundry room, if you'd prefer."

"Wine is just fine," Brand replied, pointing at the fridge.

"In there?"

Feeling relieved, Patrick nodded. "Yeah. Thanks." While he filled the vase with water, he checked the timer. He had just over twenty minutes and spotted the low simmer of the water in the pot on the stove. "The corkscrew is in the drawer to the left of the dishwasher," he told Brand as he placed the flowers in the vase, then set both on the table.

"The glasses?"

He pointed at a cupboard, and Brand crossed to it.

Patrick found himself maneuvering around Brand's bigger body to grab the linguini noodles and add them to the boiling water. At the same time, his date pulled the stemware from the cupboard he'd indicated. The dance felt domestic and surprisingly easy . . . even though his guest took up a lot of space.

Once Brand had everything, he retreated to the other side of the kitchen bar to pour their drinks.

With the noodles boiling, Patrick pulled out the bowl of cauliflower he'd cut into chunks. He'd already sliced tabs of butter on top. Wrapping the bowl with a paper towel, he placed it into the microwave and pressed the veggie button.

A few seconds later, the microwave started.

"What was that?" Brand asked from where he stood. Once he had Patrick's attention, he pushed one of the filled stemware across the counter toward Patrick.

Patrick crossed to his side of the counter and rested his hip against it. "Thanks," he said, picking up his drink. Before taking a sip, he explained, "Once the microwave dings, it'll be cauliflower steamed in butter. A soft, tasty vegetable to go with the parmesan over a bed of linguini."

Brand hummed, his expression one of anticipation. "Sounds fantastic."

Swallowing his mouthful of merlot, Patrick smiled at the man. "It will be." Then he winked. "There's salad, too, but don't fill up on all that. Just like I promised, there's tiramisu for dessert."

Tipping his head back, Brand groaned. He rubbed one hand over his flannel-covered stomach. "Oh, man. Patrick," he whined. "That all sounds so damn good. When?"

Patrick laughed as he pointed toward the timer on the oven. "Ten minutes, big guy."

Brand swallowed so hard his Adam's apple bobbed. "Okay." He swallowed a gulp of wine. "I can wait." Even as Brand said the words, he fixed a gaze so full of longing on Patrick's oven.

Shaking his head, Patrick pointed toward the already-set dining room table. "Have a seat, Brand. I'll start you with the salad."

Immediately, Brand's expression shifted to hope. "Yeah?"

Patrick couldn't believe how excited Brand became over the prospect of food. "Yeah. Absolutely." After setting his wine back on the counter, he crossed to the refrigerator. Patrick pulled out the bowl of salad with one hand and used his other to grab a couple of dressings—one ranch and one creamy Italian. "So, you can't cook, but you love food." As he took the items to the table, Patrick asked, "Did you ever consider taking a cooking class or something?"

Even as Brand's lips pinched, he nodded. "Yeah." As he glanced between to bowl of salad and Patrick's face, a hint of embarrassed reddish hue filled his cheeks. "I got kicked out."

Patrick almost dropped the salad dressings in surprise. "Wow? Really?" When Brand nodded, he couldn't help but ask, "Why?"

CHAPTER FOUR

Brand's face felt on fire. As much as he wished he could have kept his mouth shut, he didn't lie. He prided himself on that, even when it made him uncomfortable.

Instead, Brand would rather be straight up and declare he wasn't going to answer something.

Clearing his throat, Brand watched as Patrick placed a heaping serving of salad into his bowl. He admired the dark-green lettuce, the orange, red, yellows, and greens of the thinly sliced peppers, as well as the white of the blue cheese crumbles and onion strips. He made out chunks of hard-boiled egg, plus the pale-green of pepperoncini.

"Wow," Brand murmured appreciatively. "This has everything." He quickly grabbed the Italian dressing and poured a healthy dollop on top of his greens. "Thank you."

Patrick served himself, then grabbed his wine from the counter before re-joining him. "You're welcome." He pointed at the items on the table. "You're also welcome to add some toppings. I have croutons, fried onions, fried jalapenos, and sunflower seeds."

Brand finally focused on the array of pouches and canisters lining the table. "Damn. Thanks, man." Humming appreciatively, he began grabbing each in turn and pouring a little bit onto his salad. As Brand started mixing everything, he heard the beep of the oven timer. Watching Patrick rise, he realized the man had used serving the salad to distract him from his stomach . . . and his whininess. "Sorry. I know I can get a little . . . irritable when I'm hungry."

Shrugging, Patrick slid oven mitts onto his hands, then opened the oven door. "It's no problem. I'm glad it worked."

As Patrick bent over and reached into the oven, Brand found his gaze sliding over the lean man's sexy bubble butt. It was showcased exquisitely in the nice jeans he wore. He wondered what it would look like without clothes. Brand bet it would be a thing of beauty.

Feeling his blood flood his already half-hard prick — *the guy really is sexy* — Brand returned his focus to his food. He needed a distraction.

Right. Patrick had asked about the cooking class.

"So, uh . . . I met Vance about thirteen years ago now," Brand started slowly, trying to explain. He speared a forkful of salad. Before shoving it into his mouth, he admitted, "My dad is pretty old school, and my parents had very strict gender roles. My dad brought home the bacon, and my mom cooked it."

Patrick winced but didn't reply as he drained the noodles.

Brand watched for a second as Patrick next pulled the cauliflower dish out of the microwave and gave it a stir. For some reason, he found the man's smooth, sure actions fascinating to watch. When Patrick moved everything to the counter and began fixing their dishes, glancing up at Brand in the process, Brand returned his focus to his food.

"When I met Vance, it was super eye-opening," Brand told Patrick as he gathered another bite of food. "He was the one who cooked in his marriage, and you've met him. He's in no way effeminate." Snorting, Brand shook his head. "I couldn't believe it."

Carrying a plate of food in each hand, Patrick returned to the table. He set one that was nearly overflowing to the left of Brand's salad bowl. As Patrick crossed to his own setting and rested his plate nearby, Brand admired the offered food.

Brand's mouth watered. The chicken parmesan lying on a bed of noodles looked and smelled delicious. The cauliflower appeared soft and buttery. Brand could hardly wait to dig into it.

"So you didn't learn to cook as a child because of your upbringing," Patrick summed up.

Brand swallowed the bite of food he'd shoved into his mouth, then took a sip of wine. Nodding, he explained, "Between watching Vance in his marriage and recalling my own parents' relationship, I kinda swore off all that shit." Realizing what he'd just admitted, Brand paused in his eating and stared at Patrick. "Um, I—"

Patrick snorted softly. "Didn't mean to say that, did you?"

"Hell no," Brand mumbled.

Leaning one forearm on the table, Patrick edged toward him. "Tell you what. I'll let you off the hook on that one for now, and you continue your story about your lack of cooking skills."

"Thank you," Brand replied on a deep sigh. Telling someone you're on a first date with that you didn't do relationships— *Ugh. Totally bad form.* Even a socially inept guy like Brand knew that. "So, he tried to teach me to cook a little bit, and when I was with him, everything turned out fine." Recalling those lessons, Brand shook his head. "Anytime I tried to do it myself, however, something always went wrong. I'd forget about it and burn the water, overcook noodles, mess up the spices. Sometimes the meat was too raw. Other times it was overdone." Brand sighed deeply. "Even when I used timers I still botched things up. For years, I gave up. If it wasn't a frozen meal, I didn't eat it."

"Wow. Damn." Patrick stared at him, his gaze sliding up and down. "You look pretty darn good for a guy who's been living on crap."

Brand laughed before shoving the last bite of his salad into his mouth. As he chewed, he set the small plate aside, then slid the meal plate toward him. After he'd finished swallowing, Brand waggled his brows at Patrick.

"Thank you, Patrick. You're pretty damn cute yourself." Brand liked the way Patrick's cheeks took on a pinkish hue and how he lowered his chin to peer at him through his lashes. *So damn pretty.* Brand didn't know if men wanted to be considered pretty, so he kept that thought to himself. "Naw, I suppose I exaggerated. My mom brought me alotta meals, and Vance did, too . . . especially after my ma died. It wasn't too often that I had to resort to cardboard meals."

"Oh, god," Patrick murmured, his eyes widening. "I'm sorry. How long ago was that?"

"A little over three years ago," Brand told him. He couldn't help the way he smiled wistfully. "She was an amazing mother."

Patrick reached out and touched his arm, resting his palm on Brand's forearm. "I'm sorry."

Brand rested his free hand over Patrick's, surprised at how nice the gesture felt. "Thanks, but it's okay." He met the other man's gaze and gave him a smile. "I've accepted it, and I've done my grieving. As much as I miss her, *this*" —he squeezed Patrick's hand, silently indicating men dating other men— "she wouldn't have understood." Grimacing, Brand admitted, "She often wondered how I could be okay working for a man who was openly gay . . . first Laramie's Uncle Damian, then Laramie." Seeing Patrick's parted lips and wide eyes, he quickly added, "Don't get me wrong. She thought they were nice men, but she didn't understand how they could be the way they were." Brand grimaced. "Dad, on the other hand—" He snapped his mouth shut and shook his head. "I really don't want to talk about him."

"Not in your life anymore?" Patrick mused softly.

On reflex, Brand tightened his fingers over Patrick's own. "No." He knew that single word sounded forced. He couldn't help it. Seeing Patrick's wide-eyed stare, Brand grumbled, "He's turned into an ass." He twisted his lips as he returned his focus to his food. "Well, *more* of one."

Just as it always happened, when Brand thought of his father, his appetite waned. There was nothing more detrimental to his desire for food than thinking of his asshole father. When he'd been a kid, Brand had remembered the man being fun-loving and happy—taking him to sports games and throwing a football with him—that had all changed by the time Brand had hit his late teens.

Brand had decided to go into animal husbandry, and his father hadn't thought that was a real man's job. It didn't matter that all the teachers and vets teaching the courses were men, too. His father had told him to skip college and come work at the steel company with him. Brand had refused, and his father hadn't talked to him much ever since.

After so many years, Brand didn't understand his father's prejudices, so he didn't try to. Instead, he'd created his own life . . . his own family.

With Brand's focus on Patrick, he wondered if the kind lawyer before him would play a role in his future. He sort of hoped so. Not only did Patrick seem to be a nice guy, but if Brand could get his head out of his ass, he could admit to himself that Patrick was hot as hell.

Patrick squeezed Brand's wrist again, making him realize they still held hands.

Clearing his throat, Brand offered a wry smile, then released Patrick. He couldn't deny the disappointment he felt when Patrick did the same. With his arm free, Brand spun the tines of his fork in the saucy linguini.

"So, uh . . . anyway," Brand began again, doing his best to move past the awkward moment. "After I failed to reproduce even the most basic of Vance's recipes"—Brand hated failing, and he growled—"Vance suggested a cooking class."

"So you took one?"

Brand nodded, chewing a bite of succulent chicken, cheese, marinara, and noodles. "Oh, fuck!" he mumbled around his mouthful. "So damn good."

One thing was for certain. Not being able to cook for shit caused Brand to enjoy every amazing thing he put in his mouth. He couldn't think of anything better than filling his belly with an enjoyable, home-cooked meal.

While Brand liked going to a restaurant as well as the next man, he thought home-cooked shit was better. He knew exactly what was in it and could adjust the rest of his day's food intake to accommodate the extra calories. Brand loved exercise, so he didn't mind. Plus, wrangling and feeding pigs was a full-body activity.

Patrick chuckled softly. "So glad you like it."

Brand paused long enough to flash a grin Patrick's way. Then he went back to eating. To his pleasure, his date didn't seem to care. For the next ten minutes, Brand gobbled the incredible food Patrick had made for him.

Once his stomach no longer ruled his thoughts, Brand slowed his hand's plate-to-mouth movements. He scooped up another forkful only to pause with it resting over the plate. Sighing, he turned his attention back to Patrick.

As Brand watched Patrick chewing slowly and eyeing him carefully, he felt a little heat rise in his cheeks. "Uh, sorry. Was good."

Patrick smiled as he took a sip of his wine. His gray eyes twinkled with his pleasure . . . and maybe even a little warmth. Returning his glass to the table, Patrick returned his regard.

"I'm so very glad you liked it," Patrick told him softly. "There is no greater compliment to a chef than taking away the recipient of their food's capacity to focus on anything but their creation."

Brand took a second to process that. Then he gaped. When Patrick did nothing but continue to smile at him, Brand licked his lips and swallowed.

"Really?" Brand couldn't help himself. He had to ask.

Patrick immediately nodded, still smiling. "Oh, yeah. Absolutely."

Brand couldn't find a hint of guile in the man's face. Still, he had to ask, "Do all chefs feel that way?"

Shrugging, Patrick tipped his head back and forth a couple of times as if contemplating his answer. "Well, I can't speak for all of them. After all, I'm not *actually* a chef, but I can tell you I sure find it flattering." Winking, Patrick flicked his gaze pointedly at Brand's plate before reminding him, "Remember to save room for dessert, big guy."

For some reason, the way Patrick said *big guy* made Brand want to preen. There wasn't a hint of derision in his tone. Instead, it sounded like a compliment . . . as opposed to something derogatory from a bully or a come-on from a flirty lady.

"Right," Brand replied, nodding. He couldn't fight his grin. "Tiramisu. Yum!"

Brand had never had home-made tiramisu and couldn't wait to try it.

Patrick laughed, then lifted his fork and pointed it at Brand's plate. "Don't feel like you have to finish, but you should know, I have plenty." Then he lowered his voice to a sultry tone. "And if you ask real nice, I might just make you a doggie bag."

Freezing with his fork halfway to his mouth, Brand couldn't stop the way his eyes widened as he focused on Patrick. His heart rate spiked in his chest, and beads of sweat warmed his temples. He sucked in a harsh breath.

Was Patrick insinuating what he thought he was insinuating? Was his date asking for sex?

Even though Brand's dick grew hard in his jeans at the

thought of getting some attention, Brand didn't know if he could go through with it. He'd never had sex with a man before. There was no way he wanted to allow Patrick to sink his cock into his ass, so how could he ask the other man to do that?

"Uh . . ."

"Oh crap," Patrick muttered as his eyes grew wide. He lifted his free hand in placation. "I'm sorry. That totally came out wrong. I didn't mean sex or, uh . . . or anything." His cheeks took on a scarlet hue. "Not that I don't want to with you, um, eventually. Just not" — he shook his head — "no sex tonight."

"Does that include blowjobs?" The words were out of Brand's mouth before his brain could catch up. It was his turn to blush. "Aww, fuck. Guess I shouldn't have said that." Putting down his fork, Brand heaved a sigh as he rested his forearms on the table on either side of the plate. Before Patrick could respond, Brand told him, "Look. I'll be straight with you. I've never had sex with a guy, but I've had a few blowjobs in the back room of The Red Door, and I enjoyed 'em. I don't know if I could do more than that, but I find you attractive, and I think you're a nice guy. I—"

Brand paused, hesitating.

Am I really going to admit this?

"I've never been in a relationship, so I'd like to keep it discreet . . . at least for a little while." Brand scowled as he shook his head even as he continued to meet Patrick's gaze. "Not from friends, of course . . . like Vance and, uh" — he waved his hand absently in the air — "whoever your friends are, I guess."

Patrick nodded slowly, a smile slowly beginning to curve the sides of his lips. "Okay. I think I'd like that, too."

Happy to hear that, Brand grinned broadly. As he lifted another forkful of food to his lips, he admitted, "And I was kicked out of the cooking class because I set the chef's arm on fire."

As embarrassing as the episode had been at the time, hearing the sound of Patrick's laughter almost made it worth it.

God, that's a damn nice sound.

CHAPTER FIVE

Unable to help himself, Patrick laughed out loud. He covered his mouth, trying to stem his flow of chuckles, but the smirk on Brand's face as he shrugged and continued to eat didn't lessen his mirth. The fact that Brand snorted softly told Patrick the man wasn't upset at his reaction.

Patrick guessed he'd probably expected it. Brand was maybe using it as a tension icebreaker. As much as Patrick appreciated his date's openness, talking about expectations, relationships, and sex was tough.

Getting himself together, Patrick still snickered even as he murmured, "Sorry." His cheeks felt hot, but he ignored it. For some reason, in Brand's presence, Patrick had been blushing a lot, but he intended to dwell on why another time. "So, um, how did you manage that?"

There has to be a story behind that statement.

Brand finished chewing the last bite of his food. Putting down his fork, he patted his stomach and hummed. He grinned as soon as he could.

"That was amazing. Thank you." Brand let out a happy sigh, looking extremely comfortable. "I'd ask for the recipe, but it would just be a disaster." Then Brand rolled his eyes and admitted, "We were supposed to be searing chicken fillets. I somehow got the pan way too hot and just as the chef came over to see why my oil was starting to smoke, it flared into a fire and set his sleeve on fire." His lips curved into a pained smile as he continued, "Of course, being the moron in the kitchen that I am, I mixed up baking powder and baking soda."

"Oh, god!" Patrick cried, imagining the mess. "You dumped baking powder on his sleeve?"

Groaning, Brand nodded. "And on the pan, too." He lifted his hands, splaying his fingers, and made an explosion noise.

Patrick smacked his forehead lightly as he imagined the carnage. "Did the chef end up okay?" he asked, rubbing his face . . . then his arm as imaginary fiery tingles caused his skin to prickle.

Brand nodded again. "Yes, thank god. Fortunately, one of the women in the class grabbed a fire extinguisher while another guy grabbed this big bag of pink Himalayan sea salt." Sighing, he explained, "While the lady hosed down the chef, the guy doused my frying pan." Lifting his hands, palms up in a *what are ya gonna do* motion, Brand finished, "And understandably, the chef didn't want me in his class anymore."

"Just from that one incident?" Patrick thought that sounded a little harsh. "Anyone could make that mistake."

To Patrick's surprise, Brand's face turned beet red. His lips pinched, and he shook his head. "That was the *third* class and just the culmination," he muttered. "The first class, I dented the chef's fancy wok." Lifting his hands, Brand told him, "I still don't know how. All I did was drop it, but it must have banged against the corner of the stainless-steel counter just right. I paid for it, of course, but—" Brand shrugged.

Patrick winced in sympathy, and Brand continued.

"Then, the second class, I dropped a bag of flour."

Sighing, Patrick shook his head. "And it broke?"

Brand nodded.

Reaching over, Patrick patted his hand. "Duly noted. You're a terror in the kitchen."

"Afraid so." Brand pointed at the empty plate before him. "Which is why I appreciate your efforts so damn much."

Patrick was glad he'd made a double batch, which allowed

him to offer, "I have plenty. I'll send some home with you." Without waiting for a response, he rose to his feet and grinned. "I'll also send some dessert with you if you end up liking it. Are you ready for tiramisu?"

Brand's dark eyes widened, and he licked his lips. "Hell yeah."

Laughing at the enthusiasm in Brand's voice, Patrick crossed to the refrigerator.

Patrick relished the easy conversation between himself and Brand. They talked about his own family and steered clear of Brand's father. Everything about the man had pretty much already been said.

Prick.

Brand asked how Patrick had gotten into his line of work, and Patrick told how he'd loved his own childhood and had wanted to help kids have that same opportunity. Due to client privilege, he couldn't tell much in the way of stories. Patrick did share about his college years, and he admitted he felt very grateful to his mother and her head for numbers.

"Without her foresight and planning, I would have ended up with exorbitant student loans just like many of the other schmucks in my class," Patrick had told him, shaking his head. "I heard one guy graduated with thirty thousand in student loans and ten grand in credit card debt. How do people start a life like that?"

Brand had shrugged. "I worked all through school, so I don't know. I delivered papers in the AM, then worked as a stock boy in the evenings for a warehouse store." He'd lifted his arms and flexed. "Helped me hone my muscles, which was really nice once I started dealing with pigs at Laramie's farm." He tipped his head back and forth as he amended, "Well, it was owned by his uncle back then. Damian Goshen. Good man."

Later, Patrick was surprised when Brand insisted on helping with clean-up when he started making up his *to go* containers.

"Oh, no, man," Brand stated, carrying their plates to the sink. "It's only fair. You cooked. I clean." With a wink, he added, "Promise I won't break anything. I'm good at cleaning."

Deciding to let the man have at it, Patrick lifted his hands in surrender. "Okay. I'll get some containers filled for you."

Brand growled softly as he eyed the leftovers. "Thanks, Patrick."

Patrick bit back his snicker. The man loved his food. He cast side-eyed glances Brand's way as they worked around each other, unable to help but admire the big man. Brand cut a fine figure in his form-fitting flannel shirt and faded jeans. Somehow, the thin, short-sleeved material seemed to cling perfectly.

As Patrick finished sliding two-thirds of the remaining tiramisu into a large plastic container, his focus slid over Brand's brawny arms. His guest's muscles flexed and relaxed under his skin as he rinsed dishes and placed them in the dishwasher, teasing Patrick's desire to touch. His blood heated anew and flowed south, and Patrick couldn't help but wonder what Brand's skin would feel like under his palms. He longed to know how Brand's strong arms would feel holding him.

Was Brand a gentle lover? Or would he use his strength to hold him down and take what he wanted?

Patrick felt a shudder ripple through him when the thought slipped into his mind of being tied to his bed and Brand having his way with him. He'd only been with a few lovers that had been willing to indulge in Patrick's fetish — either because of lack of trust on Patrick's part or from lack of interest on his boyfriend's. He bet Brand could rock his world so good.

"Is everything okay?"

Brand's softly spoken question yanked Patrick out of his musings. He swallowed hard, then managed to smile as he met the other man's questioning gaze. For an instant, Patrick thought he spotted an answering heat in Brand's eyes, but then it was gone.

"Y-Yeah." Patrick cleared his throat. "Sorry. Just thinking."

"About—" Brand cocked his head. "Or maybe I don't want to know?"

Patrick opened his mouth, then closed it again, uncertain how to respond. Since it was an honest question, however, he figured Brand deserved an answer. "About something personal that I'm not willing to share quite yet." Seeing Brand's confused concern, he added, "I will once we get to know each other better, though."

"Sounds good," Brand replied softly. Then his gaze fell to the containers. "Wow. You sure you want to give me all that?"

Nodding and grinning, Patrick felt relieved to be back on safe ground. "Oh yeah. I don't need all those extra carbs." He patted his lean stomach. "Unlike you, I have a desk job, and I have to work damn hard to keep this flat belly."

Brand's gaze strayed to Patrick's stomach, then lower before sliding his focus back up his body. There was no mistaking the flash of heat in Brand's eyes that time. The look seemed to make his dark eyes glow.

Then Brand blinked, and the moment was broken. "I think you look amazing," he murmured huskily before glancing around the kitchen and dining room. "Did I miss anything?"

Patrick shook his head. "No." He realized their time was at an end, and disappointment filled him. Casting about for an idea to extend their time together, he opened his mouth.

Brand beat him to speaking, however. "Guess I better get out of your hair then. Thank you again for dinner."

"You're not in my hair," Patrick quickly countered. *Especially not the way I wish you would be.* "I had fun. Thank you for coming."

Picking up the plastic bag that he'd placed all the containers in, Patrick held it out to Brand. "In fact, I hope we can do this again sometime."

And maybe more.

"I'd like that, Patrick," Brand replied, his tone soft. His dark-eyed gaze again swept over Patrick's body as he took the offered bag. "Can I call you tomorrow?"

Patrick immediately nodded as he began leading the way back through the house to the front door. "I'd like that."

Once they reached the door, Brand set the bag down and picked up his hat, which he placed on his head. He reached for his coat.

Girding up his courage, Patrick blurted out, "Did you mean what you said when you arrived and called this a date?"

Brand paused and turned to face him. "Yeah. I always mean what I say."

"Then how about a good night kiss?"

As Patrick made the offer, he felt heat creep up his neck to his cheeks. When he saw Brand's focus slide to his mouth, he licked his lips on instinct. Patrick watched Brand's nostrils flair as he again met his eyes.

"I told you before," Brand whispered, his voice sounding deeper than it had all evening.

It sent a shiver of longing down Patrick's spine.

"I've only dated a handful of times and always women. You don't normally kiss a girl on the first date." Brand eased closer, his deep brown eyes giving him a piercing stare. "But I'd sure like to taste your mouth."

Patrick bit back a moan as Brand reached for him. He willingly slid a step forward, meeting him halfway. Lifting his arms, he rested his hands on Brand's broad chest, and when Patrick felt the bigger man gently cradle his hips, the skin of his groin and thighs goose bumped.

As Brand began dipping his head, he rumbled, "You'll tell me about other differences between dating a woman versus a man as they come up, too, right?"

"More than happy to share," Patrick replied, his brain shutting down as he focused on Brand's mouth.

Brand grunted in acknowledgment, then pressed his mouth on Patrick's. His touch was soft, tentative even. He slid his lips against Patrick's as if searching for the proper placement.

Patrick met his touch, pushing into the contact. He eased his lips apart so he could touch his tongue to Brand's lower lip. The move seemed to surprise Brand, as for an instant, he froze.

Then Brand lifted a hand to cradle Patrick's nape while his grip on his hip tightened. He tipped his head, slotted their mouths together more fully, and took control of the kiss. Thrusting his tongue out, Brand dipped it into Patrick's mouth, sweeping around his cavity, teasing, touching, and tasting.

Gripping Brand's shirt, Patrick groaned softly. He met the man's aggression, reveling in the tongue-play, chasing Brand's appendage with his own. Nipping and lapping, Patrick fell headlong into the exquisite act of kissing Brand.

Brand fed Patrick a growl, causing fire to course through Patrick's veins. The way Brand's hand slid from his hip so he could wrap that arm tight around his waist, flushing their bodies, drew another moan from Patrick as his nipples beaded. Even how Brand slid his other hand around to grip his nape, dominating him, created the most delicious of tingles to course through him.

Patrick didn't know when it had happened, but he suddenly felt the wall pressed against his back. Brand's hand slid from his waist to his ass. Squeezing Patrick's cheek, Brand lifted him.

Acting on instinct, Patrick spread his legs and wrapped them around Brand's waist. He felt the press of the bigger man's bulge against his own hard erection and moaned. A shudder of pleasure rocked through him, and his hips thrust once, twice, before he could bring himself under control.

Brand broke the kiss and lifted his head, meeting Patrick's gaze with an expression that appeared hungry . . . almost feral. His dark eyes gleamed with intensity as he stared down at him.

"I was trying to be good," Brand told him, his voice raspy with obvious desire. "I was gonna ignore my hard dick and walk out the door. But you wanted a kiss." Growling, Brand dipped his head and pressed another slow, sipping kiss to Patrick's mouth. "Now I don't wanna leave. Want relief." Brand rocked his hips, rutting against Patrick. "Feel your hard cock. Do you want relief, too? Tell me I can touch you."

Patrick slid his hands up to Brand's shoulders and wound them around his neck. "Hell yeah, Brand," he murmured. He would have felt bad about how needy he sounded, but feeling Brand's continued grinding, he knew the other man was in the same boat. "Want me to suck you?" Patrick's mouth watered just at the idea.

"Not this time."

A mixture of disappointment and anticipation filled Patrick. As much as he would have loved to get an up close and personal visit with Brand's erection—he just knew it would be exquisite—he couldn't wait to see what the other man had in mind. Plus, Brand had said *this time.*

That means he plans to do this again.

When Brand pulled Patrick away from the wall and began carrying him out of the foyer, he held on tight. His heart thudded in his chest as he relished Brand's show of strength. Patrick found it almost as sexy as his kisses.

Then Brand dropped back onto Patrick's sofa, leaving him

straddling his lap.

Patrick gathered enough brain cells together when he felt Brand working his fly. Leaning back, he watched with bated breath as his new lover opened his jeans. When Patrick reached to do the same to Brand's, the other man growled and let him at it.

A second later, Brand pushed down Patrick's underwear. His groan was nearly drowned out by Patrick's gasp.

"Commando," Patrick whispered in awe as Brand's long, thick cock pressed beneath the flaps.

"Oh fuck," Brand mumbled. "So fucking sexy."

Then Patrick felt Brand's fingertips glide over the piercings in his dick, and he struggled to keep his eyes from rolling back in his head as tingles erupted through his groin.

Chapter Six

Brand had never seen cock piercings . . . not in real life anyway. The startling sight caused his heart rate to spike and his mouth to water. Having never sucked a dick in his life, his response startled him.

Still, his desires for this first round were simple. His balls needed relief in the worst way. He wouldn't be able to put his desire off for long.

That didn't stop Brand from gently fondling each of the Jacob's Ladder's five balls. Once he reached the top, he teased his fingertip around the hoop of the Prince Albert piercing. His index finger was so thick, he couldn't slide beneath it, but that didn't seem to matter to Patrick.

The way Patrick moaned and trembled in his hold made Brand feel ten feet tall.

Lifting his gaze from Patrick's leaking dick, Brand focused on his face. The heavy-lidded expression on his new lover was a thing of beauty. With the way his cheeks were flushed and how he panted with every breath, Brand thought the man appeared absolutely stunning . . . and dick-throbbing handsome.

"You're gorgeous," Brand mumbled as he wrapped his fingers around Patrick's cock.

Instead of jacking it, he rested each fingertip on a ball and gently massaged them. The way Patrick's fingers dug into the flesh of Brand's shoulders—even through his shirt—as well as how he rocked his hips was very telling.

"You mewl so very nicely." Brand relished the noises escaping Patrick's mouth. He loved knowing how he affected the other man. "I could get you off just like this, couldn't I?"

"Yessss," Patrick hissed as a shudder worked through his body. A whine escaped him next. "Brand, please!"

The move caused Patrick's groin to jostle against Brand's own balls and the base of his engorged dick. Sparks shot through his testicles, and the zing at the base of his spine told him he didn't have long. The exquisite way Patrick's lean body caused his blood to burn enflamed Brand's senses, and he couldn't wait to explore more.

"I bet if I tied you to the bed and played with your dick, just like this, I could get you off, couldn't I, Patrick?" Brand had never spoken so bluntly to a lover, but then again, he'd never had a male lover before.

Hook-ups in a dark club didn't count.

To Brand's pleasure, Patrick's eyes widened behind his black frames. The gray appeared to darken to the color of thunderheads. Patrick's face somehow managed to flush even further as his panting sped up.

"Y-Yeah," Patrick mumbled. "God, yes."

Brand grinned. "Oh, I like that response. But first."

Ignoring Patrick's groan when he released the smaller man's dick, Brand wrapped his arm around the man's waist. He pulled him close, causing him to sprawl over Brand's torso. With his other hand, he threaded his fingers through Patrick's hair.

After releasing Patrick's waist, Brand slid that hand down the back of the man's jeans. He cupped Patrick's ass cheek and squeezed experimentally. The firm mound felt perfect in his grip.

"Now," Brand rasped. "Rut on me. Spill your seed all over me. I want us soaked in our cum."

Brand didn't give Patrick a chance to reply. He used his

hold on the other man's nape to tilt his head to the angle he wanted. Then he dipped his head and captured Patrick's mouth.

As Brand thrust his tongue into Patrick, he used his hold on his ass to get the man's hips rocking. The trembling man opened to him, allowing him to plunder his mouth anew. His body moved at his urging, pliant and responsive.

Upon feeling Patrick's ball-lined dick slide against his much thicker one, Brand fed his lover a moan. The sensation of the Prince Albert catching on his frenulum sent spikes of pleasure-pain coursing through his cock. The pressure of Patrick's body pushing at his groin made his balls tighten and roll.

Brand planted his feet and rocked his hips up. He pulled Patrick tight against him with each thrust, increasing the pressure of their frotting. Relishing the weight, taste, and feel of the man sprawled over him, Brand knew he was so damn close to blowing . . . and he was loving every damn second of it.

Even expecting his orgasm, it somehow still took him by surprise. Between one heartbeat and the next, his balls squeezed his cum up his dick in a rush of blissful squirts. His abdominals seized, and his cock throbbed.

Waves of euphoria swept over Brand, sending his senses reeling. He groaned roughly into Patrick's mouth, clutching the man tight against him. When he flexed his hand again, Brand's pinky slipped deeper into Patrick's crack and glided over the edge of the wrinkled flesh of his hole.

Patrick jolted in Brand's hold, shaking and shuddering. He moaned as he jerked out of the kiss. As Patrick pressed his forehead against Brand's shoulder, he continued to twitch and tremble.

Brand felt more wetness seep between them, and he growled his satisfaction. Feeling the small man in his arms get off was almost as amazing as his own release. Sighing deeply, Brand relaxed against the cushions.

Massaging the sweet mound in his palm, Brand hummed. The lethargy created by an awesome orgasm seeped over him. Turning his head, he nuzzled his lips against Patrick's temple.

The move caused Patrick to turn his head, so Brand pecked a kiss to his lips.

When Patrick smiled up at him, an unfamiliar surge of warmth flooded Brand. He didn't understand it, but he liked it. The way it combined with the delicious endorphins from his orgasm was different than anything he'd ever experienced before.

Is this what it's like to get off with someone you actually like? Maybe even care about?

He certainly hadn't ever stopped to hold a lover once he'd gotten off. Even with his female conquests, he'd been up and out of the bed within seconds. Maybe that should have been a tip-off that he was doing something wrong.

Brand figured he should explore his thoughts in depth . . . but at another time. With the way Patrick was staring up at him lazily, his black-rimmed glasses a little askew from the way he rested his head on Brand's shoulder, he returned his focus to the man sprawled over him. Brand smiled down at him.

"I like this," Brand mumbled, then sighed. "This is nice."

"Yeah?" Patrick replied softly. "Which part?"

While Brand figured his smile appeared a little silly, he couldn't help himself . . . nor did he even try to. "This." He flexed his fingers, sliding his digits over the smooth firmness of Patrick's butt. "And this." Brand pecked another kiss to Patrick's lips. Releasing Patrick's neck, he skimmed that hand down his lover's back, gently massaging along his spine. "And this."

"I like all those things, too," Patrick told him in a quiet voice.

"Good." Brand relaxed the back of his head against the sofa cushion. The move still allowed him to peer at Patrick out of the corner of his eye. "I wanna do this again soon," he admitted, just deciding to be blunt. "My schedule normally revolves around when the sows are going to give birth. Are you free most evenings?"

"Normally." Patrick rubbed his left hand over Brand's side. "What did you have in mind?"

Brand paused.

What do *I have in mind?*

Brand opened his mouth, then closed it again. "Uh . . . well, I can't cook for you, but I could order a pizza or Chinese." As he furrowed his brows, he met Patrick's warm gray eyes. "Wanna come over Thursday night? We could sit on the couch, watch a movie, and make out like randy teenagers."

Patrick chuckled softly. "I like the sound of that."

"Great."

Brand dipped his head and took possession of Patrick's mouth again. Kissing hadn't ever been something he'd been into before. With Patrick, however, Brand couldn't seem to get enough.

Between Patrick's responsiveness, turning his head this way and that, coupled with the fact that Brand didn't have to curb his base desire to dominate and explore hungrily, fully, Brand loved every damn second of it.

Plus the man's flavor . . . exquisite. He reminds me of the food we ate, the wine we drank, and something masculine beneath that. Fuck yeah!

When Brand's prick began to thicken anew, Brand broke the kiss. He licked his lips as he chuckled huskily. "Yeah, that's what kissing is supposed to do. Never enjoyed it much before, but you—"

Brand didn't bother finishing his thought. Instead, he dove back in and began exploring Patrick's mouth once more. His lips seemed to melt against Brand's own, gliding and sliding.

Smoothing his tongue along Patrick's, Brand kneaded his ass as he teased his other hand up and down his spine.

The way Patrick clung to him and pushed into Brand's touches were beginning to drive him out of his ever-loving mind. Just when Brand began entertaining the idea of reaching between them to play with Patrick's piercings, his lover turned his head. He groaned as he shook his head, his gray eyes dark with renewed arousal.

"Y-You okay?" Brand managed to grumble, even though all he wanted to do was keep kissing the man and touching his body.

God, I want to see this man naked and in a bed.

That was certainly a new feeling. Even when he'd taken women to bed, it had been at their instigation. For many years, Brand had felt almost asexual.

Why does this man feel so different?

"I-If you keep that up, I'm gonna beg you to take me to my bed and fuck me through the mattress."

Upon hearing Patrick's admission, Brand felt his brows shoot up. "Really?" He swallowed hard as his dick twitched. "Wow. So you, uh . . . bottom?"

Patrick looked surprised. Then he grinned and waggled his brows. "For the most part, hell yeah. I definitely *love* to bottom." He glanced toward Brand's groin before meeting his gaze again. "Especially for that huge piece of meat you have digging into me again. I can't wait to feel that plowing my ass."

Brand felt a shiver of anticipation flood him. His breathing hitched, and his balls warmed. He couldn't even say how much he wanted to feel that.

When Vance had gotten together with Jimmy permanently, Brand had once asked if it felt different to fuck a man. Vance's response had been, *"In general, yes. A man's chute is tighter, but with a partner you care about, it's more than that. It's the feelings*

between two people who truly care about each other that makes everything more intense."

At the time, Brand hadn't understood. Having shared a
simple frot session with Patrick, though, he thought he might
be starting to. Not only had the orgasm been more spectacular
than any he'd ever remembered experiencing, but he was
about ready to go again.

"Was that too blunt for you, big guy?" Patrick asked softly
as he rubbed his palm over Brand's shoulder and up his neck.

"No." Brand refocused on Patrick's face. "I want that, Patrick. So damn bad. I just—" Feeling his lover's hand gliding
along his jawline, he turned his head and offered more room
to explore as he hummed appreciatively. Brand loved the feel
of the man's soft, sure strokes. Knowing he needed to explain,
he finished, "Never done that before and would feel bad if we
did something I couldn't offer you in return."

Although Patrick continued to tease his fingertips along
Brand's jaw, around his lips, then back to his temple and over
to his ear, mapping his face, he remained silent.

Brand allowed the man the time he needed to process. He
wallowed in Patrick's exploration, relishing the intimacy of it.
The simple act was heady in its innocence.

"Have you ever thought about playing with your ass?"
Patrick finally asked, his tone soft and full of curiosity.

"No," Brand admitted. "It never occurred to me."

"Would you be averse to *me* someday playing with your
ass?" Patrick scraped the fingernails of his forefingers along
Brand's jaw, using the pressure to turn Brand's head so their
gazes clashed. "Maybe after we get to know each other and
trust each other?"

Brand hummed, giving that the thought it deserved. "I
think I may be okay with that." He wasn't certain how soon
that would be, but he wasn't an asshole. "Based on the good
relationships I've seen, we should be straightforward about
what we're looking for. Expectations. Needs. Wants." Seeing

the way Patrick's brows shot up, Brand realized what he'd said. He grimaced. "Calling what we have a relationship is a little premature, I know, but I wanted to be upfront. Honest."

Patrick grinned. "I appreciate that. And yeah, a little premature, but I like thinking that, too." Leaning up, he pecked his lips, then gave him a saucy wink. "And I also think that I could make you scream with pleasure while playing with your prostate."

Chuckling softly, Brand smirked back at Patrick. "I would love to experience that . . . someday."

His asshole clenched upon hearing those words, but his dick twitched, so he knew some part of him liked the idea.

Patrick must have felt it, for his eyes widened, and his nostrils flared. Even his hips twitched a little, causing Patrick's renewed erection to slide over Brand's.

Brand groaned. "Never got off with someone twice before," he admitted, gasping as he tightened his hold on Patrick's ass again. "Want to."

"Yes!"

More than on board with that idea, Brand reached between them. He peered at their nestled groins and admired how their hard cocks nudged against each other. They hadn't bothered to push their pants low enough to free their balls, but that didn't matter.

I'll have another chance to explore.

With that thought, Brand spat in his palm, then grabbed both their dicks. He squeezed as he began jacking them together, using his saliva to lubricate. While he would have preferred lube, he didn't have any, and he didn't want to stop long enough to ask for some.

Besides, with the way Patrick panted and moaned, rocking into his grip, Brand knew his lover didn't care. It didn't take long, which would have surprised Brand if he'd had enough brain cells to process such a thing. His balls pulled tight, and the base of his spine tingled.

Brand yanked his gaze from their groins just long enough to glance at Patrick's face. He admired how Patrick had his head tipped back. His lids were half-closed, and his lips were parted. As Brand watched, Patrick turned his heavy-lidded gaze to where Brand jacked them, and groans steadily escaped him.

"God, you're sexy," Brand rumbled.

His gut clenched when Patrick flashed him a hungry grin before returning his focus to their dicks.

Peering at their groins, Brand spotted the bead of pre-cum gleaming at Patrick's slit. He rubbed his palm over their crowns on the next upstroke, gathering it. Even hearing Patrick gasp, Brand couldn't tear his gaze away from where he pleasured them.

It caused his own dick to ooze pre-cum, and Brand growled as his balls churned.

Each time Brand spotted pre-cum, he rubbed their crowns and added the bit of liquid to their shafts.

"B-Brand. Oh!"

That was all the warning Brand received before white streams of seed spurted from the head of Patrick's dick. Feeling his lover's cock pulse against his own, seeing the evidence of the pleasure he'd given the smaller man, Brand felt his orgasm pulse through him.

In the next instant, Brand added his own mess to the space between them, soaking their shirts even further.

As Brand reveled in the heady endorphins pinging through him, he realized making messes with Patrick was damn fun.

CHAPTER SEVEN

Patrick opened the file on his computer and rubbed his temple. Glancing at the clock, he tried to determine if he could get through the whole thing before he would need to leave. He really didn't want to have to cancel his date with Brand a second time in a row.

I can make it.

Much to Patrick's disappointment, he'd had a last-minute appointment come up Thursday afternoon. He couldn't very well turn away business just because he wanted sex . . . no matter how much he wished he could. Fortunately, Brand had sounded understanding on the phone when he'd called.

When Patrick had arrived home the evening before, he'd hurried through his shower, then curled up on the sofa with a tumbler of rum and some leftovers. After he'd gobbled up his food, he'd called Brand. The man had picked up on the second ring, and much to Patrick's surprise, they'd spent over an hour chatting.

Patrick loved how free and easy their conversations always seemed to be, whether they were together or apart. It definitely gave him hope that they had something they could build on. Great chemistry only helped a couple's relationship get so far.

The weekend couldn't come fast enough.

Pushing thoughts of Brand out of his mind, Patrick focused on his work and began reading the file.

Almost three hours later — and after a short phone call to

his client—Patrick saved the file and the marks he'd made to it. He attached the file to an email and sent it back to the attorney he was collaborating with. They were attempting to hash out a custody agreement that both parties could agree with.

Hopefully, they were close.

Patrick shut down his system. As his computer powered off, anticipation began to rise within him. He smiled as he slid a few files into his satchel.

"You appear to be looking forward to something," Keith stated, drawing Patrick's attention to the doorway.

Taking in Keith Ryzor's amused expression where he leaned against his office's door frame, Patrick nodded. "You'd be right. I have plans." He mock-scowled at the senior partner of the firm. "Please tell me you're not going to try to ruin my weekend."

Keith shook his head as he grinned back. "Naw. Just checking the office for stragglers. You and I are the last ones here."

Patrick buttoned his suit jacket, then slung his satchel's strap over his shoulder. As he did so, he glanced at his watch. "Guess I better hurry, then."

Stepping backward, Keith beckoned him. "Got a hot date?"

"Yeah, actually," Patrick admitted with a grin. "I do. Meeting a guy."

Patrick left it at that. He knew Keith wasn't a homophobe. No one at the firm was. Patrick just didn't see the point of rubbing it in anyone's face.

Plus, Brand had mentioned his desire to start off discreet.

"Good for you," Keith said, patting him on the shoulder as he exited his office.

Grinning, Patrick nodded as he turned and locked his office's door. "Thanks."

They chatted about cases as they headed to the elevator, down the lift, and to the front of the building.

When they reached the front door, Patrick held the door for the senior partner.

"Hey, is that your date?" Keith asked, tipping his chin toward the left.

Patrick followed where Keith indicated, and a cold chill trickled down his spine. "No, he's not."

Keith stopped walking and turned to face him. His brows were lifted high on his forehead. "Someone you don't want to see or don't like?"

"Yes," was all Patrick had time to say before he realized Walter was close enough to overhear their conversation. *Shit. This isn't going to be pretty.* "Someone who is having a hard time taking *no* for an answer."

Narrowing his eyes, Keith nodded once. "That's too bad."

"Patrick," Walter said by way of greeting. "I'm glad I caught you here. More convenient." He rested his hand on Patrick's shoulder and squeezed hard enough for Patrick to feel it. "Come on. I made reservations."

Ow.

Twisting to the left, Patrick pulled away from Walter. "I'm sorry you did that, Walter. I already have plans." To his relief, Keith stayed close.

Walter frowned, the move turning his normally handsome face into something unattractive — or maybe that was the anger gleaming in his dark eyes. "Call and cancel. You're with me tonight."

"No, Walter." Patrick tried to keep his voice even, yet forceful. "We had one date, and we are not compatible. I don't know how much plainer I can be. Please stop calling me, and leave me alone."

When Walter began reaching for Patrick again, Keith stepped closer, lifting his hand in warning. "Walter, Patrick gave you his answer."

Snorting, Walter shook his head as he crossed his arms over his chest. "Don't get involved, buddy. Patrick is just playing hard to get." He fixed a lecherous smile on his face as he stared at Patrick. "It's just his way of winding me up so our night is more fun." Reaching out again, Walter made a grab for Patrick as he stated, "Now come along, baby."

Patrick growled as he batted away Walter's hand. "Leave, Walter, before I call the cops." He was beyond being patient with the guy.

Walter narrowed his eyes. "You go ahead and do that. I have friends."

"So do we," Keith replied, his voice taking on a hard edge.

Even as relief filled Patrick that his coworker and friend was coming to his aid, he pulled out his phone and opened up his directory. He kept half his attention on Walter as he did so. Patrick didn't want to feel that man's hands on him again. As it was, his shoulder hurt, and he knew he was going to have a bruise.

Holding Walter's gaze, Patrick hit the call button and lifted his phone to his ear. The phone picked up during the third ring. "Hey, Patrick. What can I do for you?"

"I have a situation I need your advice on, Detective Lewis," Patrick stated formally. He watched as Walter's eyes narrowed.

"Oh?" Carl Lewis's tone immediately turned serious. "I'm happy to help if possible. What seems to be the trouble?"

"There's a man I dated once, and now he won't leave me alone." Patrick spotted the way Walter's jaw tightened and his fists clenched. "What evidence do I need in order to get a restraining order?"

With the way Walter had shown up at his work and attempted to lead him away, Patrick realized the man wasn't going to stop on his own. He needed help. Fortunately, he knew where he could get it.

"Hmm . . . this could be a long conversation, Patrick," Carl replied. "Proof of intention to harm, and proof that you've asked to be left alone."

"Well, I have both of those," Patrick told him. "I'd like to share them with you. Can I . . . uh, hold on, please."

Patrick lowered the phone just a little and discreetly put it on speaker.

"You are such a little liar, Patrick," Walter snarled, advancing menacingly. "A cock tease and a whore. Your ass is mine until I say otherwise, or you'll be sorry. Do you understand?"

"I'm headed to my car, Patrick," Carl stated. "Where are you? Are you alone?"

The sound of the detective's voice coming through the speaker caused Walter to pause.

"I'm outside my office building, Detective Lewis," Patrick stated clearly. "No, I'm with senior partner Keith Ryzor. You're on speaker phone, detective."

"I figured as much." Carl's tone held a hint of amusement. "I'll be there in ten. I was still at the precinct. Mister Ryzor, would you be able to stay with Patrick?"

"Yes, Detective," Keith replied, still eyeing a red-faced Walter. "I'll be here."

"Excellent. See you shortly." Although it sounded like a goodbye, Patrick noticed the counter continued to climb, indicating the line was still open.

Walter, on the other hand, either didn't see that or didn't care. "You'll be sorry, Patrick. Just you wait." He lifted his hand in a manner that Patrick guessed, if he had been alone, Walter would have attempted to strike him. He stayed the action at the last second, probably because Keith stepped closer — the senior partner's six-foot-two-inch, muscular build acted as a fantastic deterrent. "I always get what I want," Walter declared. "You should have just given it to me." Sneering, he swept his gaze over Patrick's suit-clad frame. "I can't wait for you to come begging. Although, it might be fun to just take it."

"That sounds like a threat to me, Walter," Keith cut in, frowning at the man. "Care to confirm?"

Snorting, Walter shook his head. "A promise." He turned his attention back to Patrick. "You won't always have your friend at hand." Then Walter pivoted and began striding away, with his back straight and his hands shoved into his pockets, as if he didn't have a care in the world.

"Wow," Keith muttered, glancing Patrick's way. "Where'd you meet that asshole?"

Patrick sighed. "Through Richard, if you can believe it."

"Fuck!" Keith stared at Patrick in shock. "Seriously? *That's* the friend Richard said was in town?"

"Afraid so." Patrick ran his fingers through his hair as he admitted, "Richard asked if I'd go on a blind date with him. It was . . . kinda a disaster."

Keith nodded. "I bet." Crossing his arms over his chest, he commented, "But he should be going home soon, though, right? He's only visiting?"

Patrick winced. "That was what I thought, too. He's been leaving me harassing phone calls for the last five days, though." Glancing Keith's way, he admitted, "I'm actually a little uncomfortable with asking Richard when Walter is supposed to be leaving town."

"I'll ask him tomorrow," Keith told him.

"Tomorrow is Saturday," Patrick pointed out. "Why are you seeing him tomorrow?" Even though the words were nosey, Patrick didn't think anything of them. There were many instances where they had to work on Saturday.

Keith shoved his hands into his pockets, and his smile turned wry. "We have to review the Kilmer file. The father is being an asshole and refusing to agree to our client's visitation and alimony requests." Scoffing, Keith rolled his eyes. "I don't know what he's thinking. If we end up in court, we're going to take him to the cleaners."

Patrick snickered, appreciating the moment of levity. "You look like you enjoy that idea."

Grinning broadly in a way that always reminded Patrick of a shark, Keith chuckled. "Hell yeah! The father's a cheating prick who doesn't deserve the good woman he'd married." His smile turned a little chilly as he focused his attention on Patrick. "I love making those kinds of people pay."

Nodding, Patrick silently agreed.

"So, if Walter wasn't the guy you were meeting for a date, who was it?"

Patrick whipped his head around upon hearing Keith's innocently asked question. "Shit!" he hissed as he checked the time on his phone. Patrick also noticed that the numbers were still counting, indicating Carl continued to listen in. "I gotta disconnect."

"Is it safe?" Carl asked as Patrick's thumb hovered over the button of his phone.

"Yeah," Patrick immediately replied. "Keith is still here, and Walter left."

"Okay. I'll be there in two." After that, the line disconnected.

Patrick immediately called Brand.

"Hey, Pat," Brand's deep voice sounded in Patrick's ear. "Is everything okay?"

Something inside Patrick's chest warmed. Instead of assuming the worst, the man asked after him. For some reason, his tension eased.

"Sort of." Patrick found being able to be honest with a romantic interest quite a novelty. "I ran into a small problem that's delaying me, but if you don't mind me being a little late, I'd still like to see you this evening." Spotting Carl's sedan pull up nearby, Patrick lifted his hand and waved. "Uh, I gotta talk to Carl Lewis for a few minutes, but after that, can I come over?"

"Shit!" Brand cried. "You're talking to Detective Carl Lewis? Is everything okay? Are you hurt? Was there a break in? What happened?"

Patrick found himself grinning upon hearing Brand's worry-filled voice blast out a string of questions. "Yes, that Carl, but I'm fine. I promise. If I can still come over, I'll explain everything."

"Hell yeah! Get your ass over here after you're done talkin'. I wanna know what's up."

Pleased beyond anything he could describe, Patrick replied, "Thanks." After hesitating an instant, he lowered his voice and murmured, "I would really have been bummed if I had to cancel again."

"Me, too," Brand replied. "I'll keep the pizza warm for ya."

"Thanks, Brand."

"See you soon."

"Yeah." Then Patrick disconnected the call and turned his attention to Carl, who was striding toward him, a serious expression on his face.

Patrick sure hoped giving the basics to Carl wouldn't take too long. He could hardly wait to get to Brand's.

An unsettling thought hit Patrick.

What if Brand isn't interested in dealing with my problems?

His tension returning nearly ten-fold, Patrick greeted Carl, then proceeded to tell him everything.

CHAPTER EIGHT

Brand paced his front room while scrubbing his fingers through his thick hair. Even as he listened for the sound of an approaching car, he shook his head at his actions. He'd known Patrick less than a week, and already he was going out of his mind with worry for him.

Why? Why is that?

Over the years, Brand could think of very few people he'd been so concerned about. His mother, of course, had been at the top of the list. He cared about his boss, but it was a different kind of concern. Even the worry Brand had for Vance, which had caused him to force his friend to join the guys for a night out — celebrating Laramie's birthday — had come from a different place than what churned in his gut right then.

Brand wanted to see Patrick for himself and inspect every inch of him. He'd never had such alpha male impulses before, and he wasn't certain what to do with them. Would Patrick even allow him to act on them?

He was just beginning to contemplate calling Vance, to talk to him and see if he could offer a little perspective, when he heard the telltale sound of tires on gravel.

Pausing at the front window of his one-bedroom cabin, Brand pulled back the curtain and peered through the pane. As he watched, he spotted Patrick's car pass Vance's home and trundle toward his own. Releasing the curtain, he headed toward the front door.

Brand opened his door and stepped onto the porch. The planks felt a little cold under his bare feet, but he ignored it in favor of watching Patrick park. He crossed his arms over his chest and leaned one t-shirt-clad shoulder against the support pillar.

Clenching his hands into fists under his arms, Brand waited as Patrick eased from his car. His lover sported a worried crease between his brows, not quite hidden by the black frames he wore. He flashed Brand a smile, which he returned, then took off his suit jacket and hung it on a hanger that rested on a hook attached to the car's back seat frame.

Patrick finally straightened, closed both doors, and turned to face Brand.

Brand's breath felt as if it were sucked from his lungs. He thought Patrick looked so damn sexy in his slightly rumpled pale-blue dress-shirt, lavender patterned tie, and navy-blue vest and slacks. Brand noticed his lover seemed nervous.

That's not good.

For some reason, upon seeing Patrick's unease, Brand's own tension released. He straightened and uncrossed his arms. Offering the smaller man a warm smile, he held out one hand in invitation.

Answering relief flashed through Patrick's gray eyes.

With a sense of purpose filling him, Brand closed his fingers around Patrick's when his lover took his hand. He drew him up the stairs, taking a backward step in the process. Once they both stood on the porch, Brand wrapped both arms around him.

Brand relished the way Patrick immediately sank into his embrace. Dipping his head, he nuzzled the top of his lover's hair. At the same time, he used one hand to rub up and down his spine.

"You okay?" Brand had asked it on the phone and received the standard platitude in response. Now he wondered if it was true.

"Yeah." Patrick tipped his head back and peered up at him, a wry smile curving his lips. "Much better now."

Grinning, Brand couldn't resist the allure of Patrick's plump lips so close to his own. He pressed his mouth over the other man's, rubbing lightly and nibbling sensually. When Patrick opened to him, Brand dipped his tongue in and tasted the man.

As much as Brand would have loved to have kept making out, the growling of Patrick's stomach brought him to his senses. He lifted his head and grinned, liking the sheen and slight puffiness on his lover's lips caused by his kiss. Licking his own lips, Brand tasted just a hint of raspberry.

Ah, so the sheen is due in part to his lip gloss.

"Sorry about that," Patrick said, lifting a hand to Brand's face. "Forgot to wipe it off before I came." He slid the pad of one finger around Brand's lips in an obvious attempt to clean them.

Brand turned his head just a little and nipped at the tip of Patrick's finger. Hearing the other man chuckle as he pulled his hand away, Brand waggled his brows. "I don't mind a bit," he told him, winking. "Tastes good, and even better on you."

Not wanting to make a big thing of it . . . and having no desire for Patrick to change his ways for him, Brand loosened his hold. He kept one arm wrapped firmly around his guest as he guided him through the front door.

"I have the pizza keeping warm in the oven. I'll grab that while you decide what you want to drink. Sound good?" After seeing Patrick nod, Brand closed the door behind them, then waved his hand to indicate the place. "You can see just about everything from here. Living room. Dining room. Kitchen." Brand pointed at each of three doors in turn. "Bedroom. Storage closet. Bathroom. Make yourself at home."

Then Brand pressed another kiss to Patrick's temple before releasing him and heading to the kitchen.

"Can I use your bathroom first?"

Brand glanced over his shoulder at Patrick and grinned.

"*Mi casa es tu casa.*"

Patrick chuckled. "Thanks."

Watching Patrick slip into the room he'd indicated was the bathroom, Brand wondered at his offer. *My house is your house.* He didn't normally make offers like that. As he opened the oven, Brand acknowledged that his home was his sanctuary.

So why did I invite him over in the first place?

Right. I was blissed out on the endorphins caused by the best damn release of my life.

Stop dwelling and enjoy your time with your boyfriend.

Huh. I have a boyfriend? Is Patrick my boyfriend? Does he feel that way?

Brand rolled his eyes. "God, I'm having an internal debate with myself," he grumbled under his breath. "Swell."

Getting back to what he should be doing, Brand grabbed hot pads and pulled the couple of warm boxes from the oven. He placed them on top of the stove, then closed the oven door. After setting aside the hot pads, Brand pulled open a drawer and lifted out paper plates. Then he opened the top box and placed two pieces of cheesy, three-meat pizza—pepperoni, sausage, and Canadian bacon—onto one plate.

"Do you mind if I open this bottle of cabernet sauvignon?"

Having heard the bathroom door open and the sound of Patrick's soft footfalls on his hardwood floors, Brand didn't startle. "I thought you might like that, so I pulled it out of my wine fridge earlier, just in case," he told Patrick as he turned and smiled at him. "Help yourself."

Patrick hummed. "Thank you." His focus slid to the pizza. "Mmm, three-meat? Yum!"

Brand lifted his hand and slid the back of it over his forehead dramatically. "Whew! So glad to hear you say that." Lowering his hand, he indicated the food. "I do have a regular pepperoni, too, if you'd prefer."

Shaking his head, Patrick grinned at him. "No way. I'm totally making you share that awesomeness," he told him, pointing. "I'll go open this. I saw the glasses on your side-board. You want some?"

Opening his mouth to respond, Brand grew distracted. His focus riveted on Patrick's very fine slacks-covered ass. Brand heard Patrick's chuckle, and he pulled out of his admiration.

Shrugging unrepentantly, Brand finally processed Patrick's question. "No, thanks. I'm gonna have some bourbon."

Patrick nodded, and Brand returned his attention to the pizza. He slid two pieces onto the second plate, then carried both to the dining room table. Deciding he wanted something a little more informal, he crossed to the living room instead.

Brand set the plates on the coffee table, then returned to the kitchen and grabbed napkins and the pizza box. He took those to the living room, too. By then Patrick had joined him beside the couch. The open bottle of wine was on the table as well as the bottle of bourbon. Patrick held out a tumbler of amber liquid as he took a sip of his red wine.

Taking the glass, Brand tipped his chin at the liquor. "Trying to get me drunk and take advantage of me, sweet thing?"

He'd meant it to be teasing, but with the husky rumble in his tone, he couldn't hide how much the idea turned him on.

Patrick's cheeks took on a hint of pink as he peered at him through his lashes. "That hadn't been the plan, but if you're amenable—" He paused and smirked. He sobered quickly enough when he added, "Actually, I was thinking I might need a little liquid courage so I can explain what's going on in my life." Then Patrick grimaced, his forlorn gaze falling to the coffee table. "Then again, maybe I shouldn't. If I tell you and you decide you want me to leave, I need to be sober to drive." He began to lower his wine to the table.

Brand didn't know what the hell had happened that day, but he didn't like how unsure Patrick seemed. "Tell you what," Brand said, lightly gripping the other man's wrist, stopping his action. "Even if what you say changes things between us, I'll still be your friend, and I'll still let you sleep off the wine before sending you home." Brand didn't believe whatever had happened to Patrick would change what he wanted from the man, but he couldn't promise the guy that until he listened to his story.

"Come on. Sit," Brand urged, gently clinking his tumbler against Patrick's wine glass. He settled on the sofa, using his hold on the other man's wrist to urge him down beside him. "Take a load off, eat, drink, and be merry . . . all that shit."

Then Brand lifted his tumbler to his lips and took a sip. The smooth taste of the bourbon slid across his taste buds. Swallowing the mouthful, he enjoyed the slight burn as it went down his throat to settle in his belly.

Patrick remained stiff for a heartbeat, then two, before he relaxed beside him. "Okay." Then he took another sip of his wine.

Pleased at Patrick's acquiescence, Brand leaned forward and set down his drink. He grabbed a napkin and a plate. Placing the napkin under the plate, he handed it to Patrick.

"Enjoy."

"Thanks. Looks delicious." Patrick set his glass down on the coffee table, then began eating.

Brand grabbed his own napkin and plate and followed suit. For a few minutes, the only noises that filled the air were appreciative groans, soft grunts, and the pop of fingers being licked of grease and cheese. When Brand finished his two slices, he opened the box and helped himself to two more. Offering the same to Patrick, the other man lifted his index finger, indicating his desire for one piece.

After Brand served him, he resumed eating his food.

Once Patrick had finished the first two slices, he licked his fingers, then wiped them on a napkin. He picked up his wine and took a sip. With his free hand, Patrick picked up the third slice. He took a bite, then set it back down again.

Brand figured Patrick was gearing up to start talking. A moment later, his suspicions were confirmed.

Patrick took another sip of wine, then inhaled deeply. "So, I need to explain about Walter."

An unexpected rush of . . . something—*damn, is that jealousy*—flooded Brand, but he managed to keep the emotion off his face. "Okay," he mumbled around a mouthful of food. Brand smiled and nodded in encouragement.

"I went on a blind date with the man Sunday evening." Patrick winced while admitting, "The day before I met you, actually." He sighed deeply. "God, have we only known each other five days? Feels like longer."

Brand agreed, and after he'd swallowed his food, he said so. "It does." After wiping his hands, he crooked his forefingers and slid the backs of them along Patrick's jawline. He enjoyed the smoothness, betting Patrick didn't have to shave more than once a day. Even though Brand had shaved that morning, he knew he sported a five o'clock shadow already. "Feels like years, doesn't it?" It really was odd. "Why is that?"

"Sometimes it just happens that way with people," Patrick whispered, his gorgeous gray eyes darkening as he nuzzled into Brand's light touch. "It's a nice feeling, though. Right?"

Then Patrick cleared his throat and straightened, so Brand lowered his hand and grabbed his glass of bourbon. As he took a sip, Patrick stated, "Anyway, it was a disaster. The guy's an asshole, and I couldn't get away from him fast enough."

When Patrick explained about Walter's inappropriate demands to fuck him, Brand barely managed to keep the growl from escaping him. He hated feeling jealous and vowed to cement what was between them as soon as he could. Brand just hoped Patrick ended up being on the same page.

Shit! How did that happen so fast?

Brand pushed his bizarre case of possessiveness out of his

mind and focused on Patrick, who had resumed telling his story. Hearing about the harassing calls and threats was bad enough, but when his lover told him about how Walter showed up at Patrick's work and grabbed him, Brand couldn't hold back his ire any longer. An angry growl rumbled from him, causing Patrick to pause and stare at him with wide eyes.

Inhaling deeply once, twice, Brand forced himself to calm down. He offered Patrick a tight smile, knowing it probably looked a little feral. Patrick's furrowed brows and wary expression told him that.

"I'm sorry that asshole is targeting you," Brand managed to say. His voice was gruffer than normal, so he took a sip of his bourbon. After he'd swallowed, he asked, "So, you contacted Carl to report him?"

Brand needed the rest of the story. Then they could move on. He desperately wanted to touch and explore, to confirm that Patrick was truly okay.

He also wanted to reassure his lover that he still wanted him, asshole stalker or not. In fact, he felt a desire to protect the smaller male. He wondered how Patrick would feel about that.

"Yeah. One of the partners at my firm, Keith Ryzor, he was there, too, so he made a statement," Patrick told him, then he explained about trying to get a restraining order against Walter.

Nodding, Brand admitted, "I like that idea." Setting his empty plate on the coffee table, he eyed Patrick. He didn't like the uncertainty in the other man's gray eyes, especially since it was directed his way. Leaning toward Patrick, Brand rested his right arm along the back of his sofa, which allowed him to trace his fingers over his neck. "I also like the idea that when you came here, you took comfort in my embrace from the trials of your day."

Brand held Patrick's gaze as he took a sip of his bourbon.

Patrick murmured, "So, does that mean you still want to keep seeing me? Even with my problems?"

Tipping his head, Brand rested his tumbler on his thigh. "Patrick." He lightly collared the back of Patrick's neck, massaging gently. "We've had one date and a lot of fun together. I think I'd like to confirm that we're dating exclusively." Seeing Patrick's eyes widen behind his lenses, Brand felt his heart rate spike in his chest. Still, he'd always been a man to go after what he wanted, so he forged ahead. "Is that something you're interested in, Patrick?"

God, please say yes.

CHAPTER NINE

Patrick gaped. He couldn't help it.

Did I just hear what I thought I heard?

"I-I—" Patrick paused. "Really?"

"Is that so surprising?" Brand asked, his deep voice soft and soothing. "I admit I don't see what a sexy, smart, educated attorney wants with a laborer like me. Especially since I have zero experience in relationships or even being with a man." Grimacing, Brand shook his head. "God, I sound like I'm trying to talk you out of it. I'm not."

"You're educated, too," Patrick had to point out. "Just differently." He snickered, adding, "I sure wouldn't know what to do with a pregnant sow . . . or a pregnant anything."

Brand's lips curved into a wide smile, and his brown eyes lit up. "That's nice of you to say, but I barely made it through school. If it hadn't been for meeting Vance in a bar and finding out he did the same thing as what I was training for, well . . ." Brand shook his head. "I was almost flunking out. He helped me, then got me hired on here after I graduated."

"That's what friends are for. My buddy Gary helped me study, even though he wasn't interested in my field." Patrick chuckled as his tension from the day finally began to fade. With a laugh, he admitted, "I know more about acupuncture and the circulatory system than I ever wanted to."

Scoffing, Brand nodded. Then he sobered. "So, you gonna answer my question, Patrick?" As he spoke, Brand resumed his massage on Patrick's neck. His small smile spoke of his sincerity.

"I just shared how a stalker is causing problems in my life," Patrick began slowly, needing to make certain Brand understood the gravity of the situation. "He could continue to cause problems until we see if being served with a restraining order will make him go away. And your response is to ask us to be exclusive?"

"Yes." Brand's reply was firm and immediate. "I don't see the point in beating around the bush if we know what we want."

The way Brand rubbed his thumb over Patrick's pulse point caused the hairs on his neck to stand on end. It also sent tingles across his chest. He felt his nipples bead as his blood heated and flowed south.

Patrick licked his lips, holding Brand's intense gaze. "On our date on Tuesday, you said you wanted to be discreet."

"I realized that was the coward's way out," Brand told him, his brows creasing as he shook his head. His gaze flitted to the coffee table as he took a sip of his bourbon. When Brand refocused his attention on Patrick, arousal swam in his expression. "I've had time to think these last few days. I've talked a bit with friends. My request wasn't giving us the real shot we deserved."

"It's a fast turn-around," Patrick countered, still confused. The man was offering him what he wanted, but he didn't understand why. Then a thought struck Patrick. "Is this pity? I told you my tale, and now you feel sorry for me?"

Brand growled low in his throat as he released Patrick's neck. Patrick immediately felt the loss. As Brand swigged back the last of his bourbon, Patrick wondered if he had finally pressed the man too hard and pushed him away.

After placing the empty tumbler on the coffee table, Brand bent his right knee and placed it on the sofa, turning his body to face Patrick. He rested his right hand on the back of the sofa again, then reached out with his left. Gently, holding Patrick's gaze, Brand drew his hand forward.

Patrick didn't fight, and in the next instant, he found his palm pressed against Brand's jeans-covered erection. He gasped upon feeling the massive bulge. Holding Brand's hungry gaze, he felt his cheeks heat as his own body thrummed with desire for the big, sexy man he couldn't help but fondle.

"Does that feel like pity, Patrick?" Brand asked gruffly, using his own hand to push Patrick's harder against his fly. "We spent the last couple evenings talking on the phone getting to know each other as people. Now I want to get to know your body." He leaned closer as he settled his right hand on Patrick's shoulder. "Can we do that?"

As Patrick opened his mouth, intending to say *hell yeah*, Brand began massaging his shoulder. Pain spiked through him, and he winced, twisting away from Brand. A cry escaped him.

Brand immediately lifted both hands, palms out. His eyes grew wide, and he swept his gaze over Patrick searchingly. "Patrick?" Brand's tone held alarm. "What hurts?"

"Shit, sorry," Patrick replied, lifting his hand to his shoulder and rubbing lightly. "I knew I was going to bruise."

"Damn, I'm sorry, hon," Brand stated, upset creeping into his voice. "Did you tell Carl?"

"I told him Walter squeezed my shoulder pretty hard, but I didn't tell him I thought he'd injured it," Patrick admitted. "I guess I should have."

"Let's take a look." Brand rose to his feet, all traces of lust gone from his eyes as he beckoned for Patrick to stand, too. "If there's a mark, I'll take a picture, and you can forward it to him."

Patrick would much rather return to their prior activities, but he saw the wisdom in Brand's suggestion. Taking the big man's hand, he allowed him to pull him to his feet. He took an extra step so he stood flush to Brand's body as he lifted his hand and rubbed his fingers over the man's five o'clock shadow.

It was so damn sexy.

"Yes."

When Brand's brows furrowed, his eyes narrowed, and his head tipped to the side, Patrick knew he wasn't following.

Smiling, Patrick stated, "Yes, you're my exclusive date until we should decide otherwise. Got it?"

Brand's eyes widened as a big grin spread over his lips. "Got it."

Patrick rocked up on his tiptoes as he shifted his grip to Brand's shoulder. He pecked a swift kiss to Brand's full, smiling mouth, then backed up a step. "Okay. Let's get this over with."

Snorting, Brand didn't let him get far. In fact, when Patrick reached for the buttons on his vest, the other man batted them away. "Let's go to the bedroom," Brand stated, grabbing his hand. "I want to do this properly."

A shiver of anticipation coursed down Patrick's spine. His dick, which had softened upon feeling the spike of pain, once again began to thicken. The squeeze to Patrick's shoulder hadn't been the right sort of pain, but he sure looked forward to hopefully getting some of the *right* kind soon.

"What did you have in mind?" Patrick asked breathlessly as he followed Brand's guidance across the room.

"I intend to uncover each part of you myself, touching and exploring as I go," Brand told him bluntly. His dark-eyed gaze raked over Patrick hungrily. "Never explored a lover before, but I'm gonna with you. You're different."

By then, they'd reached the bedroom, and Brand stopped them at the foot of the bed. Patrick had only a couple of seconds to notice the dark furniture—a dresser, bed, and two nightstands—and the navy-blue comforter. The nightstand lamp was on, but between that and the moonlight streaming through the half-closed curtains, the overhead light was un-necessary.

Brand cradled Patrick's jaw with both hands, dipped his head, and pressed his lips over Patrick's lightly. When Brand lifted his head and peered down at Patrick, there was something deep in his eyes that took Patrick's breath away.

Affection. Wonder. Maybe even more.

Patrick couldn't find the breath to ask, and he didn't think he would have had the courage anyway.

Brand released him and took a step backward. "Your job is to just stand there," he stated as he swept his gaze over Patrick's form again.

Then Brand grabbed the hem of his t-shirt and whipped it over his head. He tossed the fabric on the padded bench that rested at the foot of the bed beside them. Next Brand reached for his fly.

Patrick could hardly breathe for the vision of masculine beauty before him. His nostrils flared, and his cock throbbed as he drank in the gorgeous specimen that was Brand. Everything about the man was sculpted perfection.

Brand's torso was wide with well-defined pectorals. His arm muscles bulged, and his abdominals were cut. The man had a fucking eight-pack!

I didn't even realize that was possible.

"What was possible?"

"God, I can't believe I said that out loud." Patrick fought against the blush threatening to heat his cheeks. "You're eight-pack," he admitted. "Never seen one in real life before."

Standing straight and tall, Brand grinned broadly at him as he shamelessly kicked off his jeans.

Shameless is right.

Brand laughed. "Figured I'd skip the underwear this time, too." He reached out and touched Patrick's chin, urging him to meet his gaze. "Do you always say your thoughts out loud when you're turned on?"

"No." Patrick's gaze flicked back to Brand's engorged cock. It was a thing of beauty—long, thick, and veiny. It had to be at least eleven inches, and Patrick couldn't wait to feel the hefty girth stretching him to capacity . . . and maybe even beyond it. "Only when I'm in the presence of a naked Adonis."

Not only was Brand's erection a thing of beauty, so was the rest of him. His long legs were roped with bulging thigh and calf muscles. Even his feet were perfect, displaying fine bones and long toes.

"So glad you approve," Brand rumbled. "Now, let's see your sexiness."

Patrick suddenly felt self-conscious. While he jogged on the treadmill several times a week, his body didn't look anything like Brand's. He managed to keep his belly flat with diet and exercise, but he wasn't muscular at all.

"Good thing I'm not attracted to guys that look like me." Brand waggled his eyebrows before he winked. He reached for the first button on Patrick's vest as he held his gaze. "I already know I'm going to find you perfect."

Upon feeling the light touch and bump of Brand's hand against him, Patrick felt his chest heave and his nipples bead. He panted softly as he peered down at where Brand touched him. By the time Brand reached the bottom button of his vest, trembles had worked through his body.

"Breathe, honey," Brand crooned. His deep voice sounded soothing and calm, yet, still somehow managed to cause a shiver to work through Patrick. "Look at my face."

Patrick snapped his focus back up to Brand's face.

His lover was smiling at him, pride gleaming in his eyes. "Do you have any idea how much I love seeing what my touch does to you?" As he held Patrick's gaze, he slid his hands up and under his vest, pushing it off his shoulders. "Never tied a tie before. Have a few, but can't tie the damn things," Brand told him, sounding a little chagrined. "Do me a favor and loosen it, hmm?"

Nodding, Patrick lifted his arms. It took him a few seconds to get his fingers to cooperate. He finally managed to loosen his Windsor and create space in his loop.

"That's enough," Brand ordered, reaching for the fabric.

To Patrick's surprise, Brand pulled the loop over his head and drew it over his own.

Patrick gasped, his breath catching in his throat. He glanced over Brand's solid frame. There was something so fucking erotic about seeing his naked lover wearing only his purple tie.

"Like what you see?" Brand teased as he began unbuttoning Patrick's dress shirt.

"God, yes," Patrick mumbled. "So fucking sexy."

Brand chuckled lightly as he made quick work of Patrick's shirt. When he reached the bottom, he pulled it from the waist of his slacks. Then he pushed it over his shoulders, and it caught on his wrists.

Moaning roughly, Brand grumbled, "I can see you tied up in your sleeves as you kneel and suck my cock."

Patrick drew in a harsh breath, then let it out on a groan of his own. "Fuck!" he whimpered. His dick twitched, and he wanted to reach around and adjust himself . . . but he couldn't, which somehow ramped up his need to a whole new level. "Brand!"

Brand growled, narrowing his eyes. Reaching down, he brazenly cupped Patrick's cock through the fabric of his slacks. "You love that idea, don't you, Pat?" Brand squeezed rhythmically for a few seconds before releasing him.

Whining, Patrick bucked his hips. "Please," he hissed.

"Not yet," Brand grumbled gruffly. "Need to see your shoulder."

Sighing with disappointment, Patrick nodded. "Let me undo these." He'd been stuck in his shirt sleeves on occasion and knew how to fix the problem swiftly enough. When Brand reached for him, Patrick shook his head and took a step backward. "Really. Please." Peering through his lashes, Patrick huskily admitted, "Let me do this, or I'm gonna blow in my slacks."

Brand groaned and grabbed his own dick. He jacked himself once, twice, then hissed and squeezed the base.

Even as Patrick made quick work of his cuff buttons, he couldn't tear his gaze from Brand's long, thick cock. As he watched, a bead of pre-cum oozed from the man's slit to drip down his wide crown. The sight alone made Patrick's mouth water, and he remembered Brand's comment.

Patrick would have loved to sink to his knees. Then the buttons of his second cuff gave way. He sighed as the release of pressure on his wrists drew him out of his lustful thoughts. *Someday soon.* After shrugging the shirt from his wrists, Patrick let it drop to the floor.

Immediately, Brand gripped the hem of his t-shirt. "Lift your arms," he ordered.

Obeying, Patrick watched with bated breath as the view of Brand disappeared, then reappeared again. He peered at the bigger man through his lashes as he slowly lowered his arms back to his sides. Upon seeing Brand's intense gaze, he barely resisted covering himself.

"You're gorgeous," Brand all but purred as he swept his focus over his torso.

Patrick began to relax . . . until Brand's gaze reached his shoulder. Brand's expression darkened, and his eyes narrowed. Giving in to his self-preservation, Patrick wrapped his arms around himself.

"Oh, honey, stop," Brand crooned, stepping close and wrapping his arms around him. Dipping his head, he nuzzled his lips against Patrick's temple. "You're fine. You're safe with me."

Feeling Brand's big palms sliding over his back's flesh, Patrick sighed and rested his hands on the other man's waist. His fingertips flexed, and he barely resisted the urge to grip the gorgeous erection near them. Patrick wanted to touch, but he needed permission.

"Patrick?" Brand purred, teasing his fingertips into the waistband of his slacks. "You with me?"

Refocusing, Patrick tipped his chin up to meet Brand's gaze. "I'm with you." He recalled Brand's crooning words and added, "I know I'm safe with you."

He wasn't certain why he felt that way, but he did.

"Good." Brand dipped his head and pressed a slow, sipping kiss to Patrick's mouth. Even though he parted his lips in the hopes of Brand deepening it, the big man eased the kiss to an end. "It pisses me off that some asshole got close enough to mark you," he stated on a grumble. At the same time, he eased Patrick backward a step. "I'm going to take a picture of it, and you're going to send it to Carl. Where's your phone?"

Patrick sighed and pulled his phone from his pants pocket. Handing it over, he tried not to fidget.

"Relax, Patrick." Brand waggled his brows. "This isn't going to stop us from having sex."

Barking a laugh, Patrick met the other man's gaze. "Hurry up, then." He cupped his hard cock through his slacks. "I'm tired of waiting."

"You got it."

To Patrick's relief, Brand made quick work of taking pictures of the growing fingerprint-sized bruises on his shoulder—front and back. Then he returned the phone to Patrick. Patrick composed a quick message to Carl and fired it off.

Chapter Ten

Brand couldn't remember a time his cock throbbed so badly. It wasn't easy ignoring it, but he did it. He had plans.

After Patrick sent the message to Carl, Brand took the phone and set it on his dresser. Then he returned to the task of undressing his sexy lover. The button easily slipped through the slot. Brand reached his hand into Patrick's pants and cupped his erection before lowering the zipper, pleased to hear the soft whiney moan the move drew from the smaller man.

"God, I love the sounds you make," Brand murmured, enjoying the sight of Patrick's flushed face and parted lips. "Love that you hide nothing from me."

Patrick peered hungrily at him, the black frames on his face not hiding any of the need glowing in his gray eyes.

Brand released Patrick's cock and knelt before him. Gripping the sides of his pants, he pushed them down as he got his first real close look at another man's dick. The long, slender, pierced rod jutted from Patrick groin—his smooth, hairless groin.

As Brand helped Patrick step out of his slacks, taking his socks with them, he couldn't tear his gaze away from his lover's bobbing shaft. While he stared, he spotted the bead of pre-cum that oozed up. It made Patrick's Prince Albert piercing gleam in the room's dim lighting.

Resting his hands on Patrick's hips, Brand used his thumbs to tease at the soft, shaved flesh. "Beautiful." He whispered the word before he could think better of it.

Wow. Never thought I'd think of another guy's dick in those terms.

It was true, though.

Brand slid one hand forward, so he could trace over Patrick's skin around the base of his cock with his fingertips. With his other hand, he reached down and carefully cupped his lover's balls. He ever-so-gently squeezed Patrick's sack while slipping his forefingers up to massage the southernmost ball embedded in Patrick's dick.

"Oh, god," Patrick muttered, rising onto his toes and arching his back. "Brand!"

Chuckling roughly, Brand eased his hold on Patrick's testicles before squeezing again. Another bead of pre-cum bubbled up from his slit. Unable to resist, Brand leaned forward, stuck out his tongue, and slid his tongue across Patrick's damp crown.

Brand lapped across Patrick's Prince Albert, pushing at the piercing, reveling in the soft whines and groans that poured from his lover's mouth. When he drew away, he licked his lips and swallowed, analyzing the flavor on his tongue—a soft hint of musk mixed with a light trace of salt. Brand liked it, so he opened his mouth and wrapped his lips around the crown so he could gently suckle on it.

"Brand! Oh, fuck!"

Patrick's cry of pleasure sent Brand's cock to throbbing. He sucked harder as he swiped his tongue over his lover's crown before teasing at his piercing. Then he slid his tongue lower and pressed against the ball embedded in Patrick's frenulum. All the while, Brand continued the gentle squeeze and release to the other man's balls.

"P-P-Please!" Patrick pleaded. "Please, please, please."

Brand wasn't entirely certain what Patrick was asking for. Still, he took his best guess. Popping off his lover's prick and releasing his sack, he squeezed the base of Patrick's dick.

"Not yet," Brand ordered, pinning a narrow-eyed gaze on

his lover. "Get on the bed, on your back," he ordered, letting go of his lover's prick.

Patrick's body swayed for an instant. His hips twitched, and his shaft bobbed. Patrick blinked once, twice, then seemed to pull himself together. He quickly scrambled onto the bed, then flopped onto his back.

Brand grinned, feeling just as eager. Rising to his feet, he fingered the tie he still had around his neck. He owned a couple, although he couldn't remember the last time he'd worn one. Years before his mom had passed, since she was the one who'd always tied them for him.

Moving to the head of the bed, Brand took Patrick's right wrist in hand. He removed the tie from his head, then slid the loop around Patrick's hand. He tightened it around his wrist before tying the loose ends around a spindle near the corner of the frame, stretching out Patrick's arm.

Realizing he probably should have asked permission — sure they'd joked about it, but actually doing it was something else — Brand swept his gaze over Patrick's face. "This okay?" he asked even as he took in his lover's heavy-lidded expression and glazed eyes.

"Y-Yeah," Patrick replied, his voice husky and soft.

Brand glanced at Patrick's cock, since a man's dick was a fantastic indicator of whether someone was truly enjoying something or just going along to please a partner. To Brand's pleasure, he saw his lover's prick hard and straining, curving proudly toward his belly. Unable to resist, Brand skimmed the pad of his forefinger along the length from base to tip.

More pre-cum oozed from Patrick as the man moaned.

Grinning, Brand quickly crossed to his closet. He found a navy-blue tie and rounded the bed. Brand made short work of tying Patrick's left hand, stretching his arm out toward the corner.

Brand thought about tying the man's legs, too, but dismissed the idea.

Maybe another time.

Rummaging in his nightstand, Brand found a condom and the small bottle of lube he used to jack off with. Then he climbed onto the bed. He rested his free hand on the inside of Patrick's left thigh and pushed his lover's legs open.

Patrick complied with the slightest of urgings, spreading his thighs wide.

Brand settled between them and put down the lube. Opening the condom, he quickly gloved up his dick. Then he tossed the wrapper to the floor.

I'll get it later.

Resting his hands under Patrick's thighs, Brand lifted them, encouraging his lover to bring his knees up and out. Once he had the other man's knees bent and resting on either side of his torso, Brand hummed at the beautiful display. Seeing Patrick all spread out for his perusal caused Brand's blood to fire through his veins in a way he'd never before experienced.

With his own dick leaking, Brand nearly gave in to his throbbing erection's need and skipped his plan. He gripped the base of his prick and squeezed, hard. Once he felt more in control, Brand released himself and returned his attention to Patrick's groin.

Brand teased his fingertips along the Jacob's Ladder, massaging each ball. With his other hand, he rubbed the Prince Albert. As he worked the piercings, he eyed Patrick's face and torso.

Patrick's chest heaved with each breath. His skin flushed. He switched between nibbling his bottom lip to opening his mouth and letting out cries of pleasure.

When Brand gently tugged on Patrick's Prince Albert, a jolt shook the man's body. Patrick arched his neck and cried Brand's name. His dick bobbed as it began to spurt.

Brand released the piercing and wrapped Patrick's dick in a loose hold. He gently massaged the balls as he watched his lover writhe with his pleasure. His seed coated the length of his torso in half a dozen milky-white streaks.

When Patrick stopped coming, Brand released him. He admired the panting, cum-covered mess of a man spread out for his enjoyment. Patrick continued to hold his legs up and out, and his arms were still tied. Sweat dampened his forehead, causing his hair to stick to his temples in places.

"Look at you, my debauched angel," Brand muttered as he grabbed the lube. "So fucking sexy."

"Please, fuck me," Patrick urged, shifting his hips a little. "Need to feel you."

"You will."

Brand poured a large dollop of slick directly onto Patrick's hole. He caught the drip with his forefingers, then teased over his lover's striated muscle. Pushing gently, Brand tried to remember everything he'd learned about stretching.

He'd gone online just two days before to research it, since he didn't want to admit his ignorance to Patrick.

Pressing his middle finger against Patrick's hole, Brand bit his lip to keep from gasping as the ring stretched and gave way. He slid his digit in as deeply as possible, pulled it partway free, then repeated the process. The tight squeeze on his finger took his breath away, and he felt his cock ooze with his anticipation of feeling that pressure around him.

"More, Brand," Patrick urged. "Please. I need you."

Brand obeyed. He pushed a second finger into Patrick, glancing up at his lover's face to see how he was doing. The man had his hands clenched around the ties. He didn't appear to be straining against them so much as using them for leverage, since at that second, he began rocking into each of Brand's finger-thrusts.

The sight of Patrick with his legs lifted, his arms spread and tied, and his muscles straining as he pushed into each of Brand's movements caused his balls to tingle. Brand grabbed his testicles and squeezed even as he continued to fuck his lover's hole. Once he felt sort of in control, he released himself so he could pour more slick onto his fingers and push a third digit into Patrick.

"Now!" Patrick demanded. "Now, Brand. God, do it now. I'm ready."

Pausing in his ministration, Brand met Patrick's glazed-eyed gaze. "Are you sure?" Brand wasn't. His dick was so much thicker than three fingers.

"I like a bite of pain, remember?" Patrick's gaze slid to his cock and the piercings there before refocusing on Brand. His eyes were clearer then. "I'm sure. Fuck me."

Taking Patrick at his word, Brand eased his fingers out. He gripped his length, using the rest of the lube to grease up his pole. His body trembled with anticipation as he grabbed Patrick's thigh.

Brand glanced at the height differences and realized he had two options — lever over the man or find a way to raise Patrick's ass. He grabbed his pillow. While using his hold on his man's thigh to lift him, Brand shoved it under his lower back and butt.

"Perfect," Brand mumbled, using the hold he still had on his dick to guide his crown to Patrick's hole. "Push out."

Then Brand pushed *in*.

When Patrick's ring immediately opened, allowing his crown to slip into the man, Brand groaned deep in his throat. He felt a full body flush as he continued to press deeper and deeper into the other man. The squeeze of Patrick's inner walls clamped onto him, wrapping his shaft in the most exquisite of pressure.

"Patrick," Brand ground out between clenched teeth as he bottomed out. Sucking air in roughly through his nose, he struggled to keep still. He knew he was supposed to give a lover time to adjust, but he didn't know if he could manage that for more than a few seconds. Each beat of his heart caused his cock to ache with his need to rut.

"You can move," Patrick told him breathlessly. "Please, please move, Brand."

Brand felt Patrick's hips shift, which snapped his focus away from where his groin was pressed flush to his lover's ass. Peering into his man's stormy gray eyes, he panted softly as he read his expression. The need staring back at him took Brand's breath away . . . and caused his dick to twitch within the confines of Patrick's body.

Patrick moaned and bucked, trying to force the issue.

Growling, Brand once again followed Patrick's urgings. He returned his focus to the gorgeous view of his thick shaft stretching Patrick's ring. Easing his cock partway out, he gritted his teeth upon feeling the rippling, massaging squeeze of his man's chute.

Brand managed to get nearly all the way out before losing control and slamming back into the man. "Patrick! Oh, fuck!" His instinct to rut, his need to claim the sexy ass on display before him, took hold. Brand grabbed Patrick's other thigh. Using his hold as leverage, he began to piston into his lover over and over.

Panting harshly, Brand couldn't tear his gaze away from where he repeatedly filled Patrick. The slap of their skin as his groin met Patrick's ass cheeks coupled with their masculine cries, filling the room with the noises of their pleasure. Patrick's hard, slender rod slapped his own belly with each of Brand's ruts, adding to the exquisite sounds that echoed around them.

Brand felt his balls tighten, and the tell-tale tingle warmed the base of his spine. Struggling to hold on so his lover came with him, he paid careful attention to the timber of Patrick's cries as he adjusted the angle of his thrusts. When Brand heard his lover scream, he noted that angle.

"There it is," Brand snarled, his balls tightening pleasurably. "Come with me, Patrick." He began pegging Patrick's prostate with each rut.

In response, as if that was all Patrick had been waiting for, his lover's slender prick erupted, again. As each spray pulsed from Patrick's crown, his chute muscles constricted around Brand's dick. Groaning, Brand sank his erection balls deep and stilled, reveling in the sensation.

The sensual massage to his length yanked Brand over the edge. "Patrick," he growled through clenched teeth as his orgasm swamped him. His senses reeled, and his seed rushed from him in mind-numbing bursts. "Oh, god!"

Black spots swam across Brand's vision as the waves of his endorphins slowly began to ebb. He peeled open eyelids he hadn't realized he'd closed and smiled down at his lover. Seeing an answering sated expression on Patrick's face, a deep wealth of smug satisfaction filled him.

Patrick's torso was covered in semen, some fresh and some already drying. His face, neck, and chest were flushed a ruddy red. However, it was the way Patrick lay lax in his bindings that Brand found truly stunning.

"Wow," Patrick slurred softly. He sighed. "Thanks."

Brand chuckled roughly. "I'm pretty sure I should say that to you." His prick began to soften within the confines of Patrick's body. While unwilling to allow the moment to end entirely, Brand still knew losing the condom within his lover would be bad form. "Relax, Pat," he urged as he lowered Patrick's legs back to the comforter.

Gripping the base of the condom, Brand eased out of Patrick's body. He immediately missed the feel of his lover's tight body and wondered how long it would be before he could enjoy it again. Brand had certainly never felt that after sex.

God, this man is amazing.

Brand swiftly tied off the condom, then tossed it in the waste bin beside his bed. Wanting to be just as marked as Patrick, he carefully pulled the pillow from beneath his man, then levered over him. He rested his weight on his left forearm, then used his right to untie first one, then the second, of Patrick's wrists.

Finally, Brand threaded his fingers through Patrick's hair and cradled his head. He sealed his mouth over his lover's. As Brand enjoyed the way Patrick immediately acquiesced to his taking, he lowered his body and pressed his weight against the other man.

Feeling the slight slide of Patrick's semen against his skin, Brand moaned into his man's mouth, relishing the idea of being marked.

Yeah, definitely doing this again soon.

Chapter Eleven

For the first time in years, Patrick didn't think about work while enjoying his weekend. He was too busy spending time with Brand. His lover invited him to stay not only Friday night, but Saturday, too.

On Saturday, Brand showed him around the farm. He took him to see the young piglets, and Patrick found holding the tiny things adorable. He'd been shocked at how soft they were.

There had been a few minutes of awkwardness when Brand and Patrick had run into Laramie and Trace. Very few people wanted to spend time with an ex-lover and his new man, even if they had ended their relationship amicably. Fortunately, Trace and Laramie had been together for several years and were secure enough in their relationship that, after the initial surprise of seeing Patrick on his farm, Laramie had welcomed him and had asked him if he had any questions.

They'd chatted for a few minutes about Laramie and his non-pig activities. The man had a few Tennessee Walking horses and offered breeding services with his stud. He also had a small herd of cows that he was expanding.

Laramie teased Brand for a moment about hiding his bisexuality. With his cheeks turning pink, Brand had shrugged and admitted that few caught his attention—male or female. Then Brand had wrapped his arm around Patrick possessively and given him a hungry look.

"Patrick is special," Brand had declared.

A blush had heated Patrick's cheeks, but he hadn't countered the big man. Instead, he'd cuddled into Brand's side. There was something he truly enjoyed about feeling his lover's arms around him in a semi-public place.

While Patrick understood the area was Brand's home, it was also a working business with plenty of others coming and going.

Sunday evening, Patrick found himself back at home and a little lonely. He missed the sound of Brand's footfalls on the hardwood floor, which were surprisingly soft for such a big man. Patrick guessed that if Brand was there with him, he would walk up behind him and wrap his arms around him.

Closing his eyes, Patrick could practically feel how it would be. Brand would rest his chin on top of Patrick's head and ask what he was making. Then he would steal a bite of whatever Patrick was putting together.

Patrick shivered as his blood flowed south. His stomach quivered under imaginary hands. He snapped his eyelids back open and shook his head.

"One weekend together and you're imagining domestic bliss."

Remembering all the words Brand had spoken about wanting monogamy and building a relationship, Patrick couldn't help himself. Brand seemed to be offering him everything he'd ever wanted on a silver platter. He worried it was too good to be true . . . as if soon the other shoe would drop.

It's just too easy.

Nothing in my life has ever been so easy.

When Patrick was with Brand, he didn't have such thoughts. It was when he was alone that his brain wouldn't stop churning, and his insecurities got to him.

The chime of Patrick's phone drew his attention. He peered at it and smiled. The text was from Brand. Just that fast, his worries evaporated.

I'll miss you in my bed tonight. Get plenty of sleep, honey.
Patrick quickly typed a response.
I already miss your big arms around me. <3 <3
Before hitting send, Patrick removed the heart emojis. It was too soon for that, right? Instead, he added a couple of kissing smiley emojis. Patrick quickly hit send before he could talk himself out of it.

A few seconds later, his phone chimed again.

Patrick spotted the kissing smileys Brand had sent back, and he grinned.

Turning his attention back to his lunch, Patrick felt happier than he had in a long time.

That happiness carried him through to the next morning . . . or maybe that could have been the texts he and Brand were exchanging.

At seven-forty-five, Brand wished him a good morning and asked if he'd slept well.

Patrick responded quickly. *Yes, I have a comfortable bed but not quite as nice as yours with you in it.*

Brand had sent him a gif of a smiley face waggling his eyebrows.

Walking into the office, Patrick couldn't keep the grin off his face. He felt buoyant. His thoughts revolved around when he could see Brand again.

Was his lover just as eager to see him?

If I ask him to come over this evening, would he?

Patrick pulled his phone out to take the plunge, but then he spotted Keith talking with Richard. Both men sported serious expressions, and Keith appeared angry. Richard must have noticed Patrick's approach, for he turned his attention on him. Keith did the same.

Under the weight of those stares, Patrick's pulse spiked.

"Good morning," Patrick greeted, doing his best to keep his voice from cracking.

"Not really," Keith replied gruffly.

Richard beckoned. "Come into my office, Patrick. We have a situation."

The hairs on Patrick's nape stood on end as he followed Richard into his office. He ignored his desire to rub his nape as Keith fell into step behind him. When Patrick heard the door snick shut behind him, Patrick's shoulders twitched with his nerves.

Patrick thought the fact that Richard was leading him to the left side of his office, which was set up with an informal, comfortable seating area, was a good thing. Then he spotted the photos strewn across the coffee table. Gasping, Patrick put his hand over his mouth as he stumbled to a stop.

Then his legs began to give out.

Keith grabbed his upper arms and urged him a couple of steps to the right and into one of the comfortable chairs spread out around the coffee table. Then the man moved to his left and took the chair there. Richard settled in one to Patrick's right.

Unable to tear his gaze away from the objects resting on the cherry wood surface, Patrick reached out a trembling hand toward them. He stopped before touching. His heart raced in his chest.

The pictures were of Patrick and Brand . . . and in them, they were naked. Most of them showcased how Patrick was tied to Brand's bed, his face an expression of ecstasy. His legs were spread wide in an open invitation as Brand fingered him.

Across each picture was written the following words — *Is this who you want representing you and your children?*

Tears burned the backs of Patrick's eyes as humiliation hit him hard. He wrapped his arms around his body, hugging himself. Whoever had snapped the photos had taken one of the most amazing moments of Patrick's life and sullied it.

What will Brand say?

Patrick finally reached over and spread out the pictures. He scanned them quickly, then scooped them into a pile and flipped them over. At least none of the pictures had shown Brand's dick, although one was of his lover sprawled over him, his broad, strong back on display, so it was clear they were fucking.

"Where did you get these?" Patrick whispered, glancing between the men.

Richard's expression appeared resigned, his jaw clenching tightly.

Keith glared at the offending items before focusing on Patrick.

"These were delivered to several of your clients this morning," Richard told him. "So far, we've had four people ask to be assigned a different lawyer."

Patrick swallowed hard. "Shit." Shaking his head, he mumbled, "I understand." Pulling out his phone, he pulled up his contacts.

"Who are you calling?" Richard asked.

"Detective Lewis," Patrick replied.

"Why?"

As Patrick hit the dial button, his brows shot up. "Because I didn't take these." He thought the answer should have been obvious, but when Richard scowled, he guessed not. "Someone is stalking me, and I have a pretty good idea of who it is."

"Told you he wouldn't have taken them himself," Keith cut in, his voice a low growl. "That's more along the lines of something *I* would do."

Patrick felt his face flush for a whole new reason.

TMI!

"Patrick? You there?"

Upon hearing Ryan's voice through his phone, Patrick returned his attention to the call he'd made. "Detective Straton?"

"Yeah, Carl is on another call," Ryan told him. "What can

I help you with, man?"

Patrick knew that Detective Ryan Straton was Carl's partner on the force, often working cases together. "Did he tell you about my altercation Friday night?"

"He did." Ryan's voice took on a gruff quality. "Your paperwork is already before the judge. We should be able to issue the restraining order by this evening. Is that why you were calling? For an update?"

"Afraid not," Patrick admitted. He scowled at the backs of the disturbing images. "I need someone to come to my office as soon as possible. Nude pictures of me with Brand were sent to some of my clients, and — "

"What the fuck?" Ryan cut in. "Who the hell would do that? Is it the same guy as from Friday?"

Patrick glanced Richard's way. The man's expression held annoyance with a hint of confusion. If his life wasn't being put in upheaval by Richard's friend, he would have felt bad for the senior partner. Except, it was *his* friend who was messing not only with Patrick, but Richard and the firm as well.

"Maybe," Patrick admitted. "But I haven't heard how they arrived at our office, yet, so I don't have all the facts."

"Okay. Carl just finished his other call," Ryan told him. "We'll be there in fifteen."

"Thank you."

"It's what we do," Ryan told him. A hard edge entered his tone. "Protect, serve, and kick ass."

Patrick felt a measure of amusement fill him, easing some of his anger. Just as he was hanging up, he saw he had an incoming call. He recognized Vance's number on his screen and winced.

"Hi, Vance," Patrick greeted, trying to keep his voice even as his gut churned with butterflies. "How are you this morning?"

"Concerned," Vance replied, his deep voice full of the emotion. "I received something this morning that I think you need to know about . . . and so does Brand."

"Damn it," Patrick muttered, rubbing his hand over his face. "How many nude shots?"

"Three. You know about this?"

Patrick sighed deeply. "Yeah. I walked into a shit-storm this morning, it seems." Glancing between Keith and Richard, he tried to figure out how the men were taking the chaos his personal life seemed to be bringing to the firm. "How did they arrive?"

"A messenger service. White's Delivery Service," Vance told him. "I saw the sign on the door as the car drove away. There was a brown manila envelope waiting on my doorstep." After clearing his throat, Vance added, "Once I realized the contents, I stopped touching the pictures. I wanted to call you before I called the cops."

"I already called Carl and Ryan," Patrick told his client and Brand's best friend. Since he was also his lover's boss, he added, "If I called Brand, would he be able to get away for a while? I can come there this evening, but I'm not sure—" Patrick paused, uncertain how to even ask what he needed to know.

Would Brand still want to date him once he discovered he was now a target, too?

"I'll tell Brand he needs to get to your office," Vance told him. "He'll want to support you."

God, I hope so.

"Thanks." Patrick cleared his throat, then added, "I'll tell the detectives that you have pictures, too."

"Good." Vance growled softly before adding, "Any help and support you need, you know you got it, right? Our friends help our own."

Patrick felt a flush of warmth. The sensation replaced the frustration, anger, and embarrassment that had been filling him. He'd only known Vance a week.

That reminded him that while Vance was contacting him as a friend, he was also a client. "Do you want your case reassigned?" Patrick had to offer.

"No," Vance replied firmly. "Naughty pictures of my lawyer shouldn't be of any consequence to my case."

"It shouldn't, but that doesn't mean some asshole might not try to use what happens in my bedroom as leverage to get what they want," Patrick explained, feeling his cheeks heat once again as his gaze strayed to the pictures. Even flipped over so he couldn't see them, the images were burned into his brain. "I just want to be sure."

Vance growled before telling him, "I have faith in your abilities, Patrick."

"Thanks, Vance."

"I'm on my way to locate Brand. I'll tell him to get to your work asap."

Sighing, Patrick thanked Vance again, then disconnected the line.

"That was another client?" Richard asked, his eyes narrowing as his focus strayed to Keith. "Who else can handle another case?"

"Vance doesn't want another lawyer," Patrick told them. Then he shared the rest of what Vance had told him.

Keith nodded. "That's the same company that brought the pictures to Tiffany's office."

"Oh, damn," Patrick muttered, groaning. "They were sent to her *office*?"

Richard nodded even as he cocked his head. "You have an idea of who's doing this?"

Patrick exchanged a glance with Keith. "You didn't tell him about Friday?"

"Didn't think it was my place," Keith admitted as he rose to his feet. "Coffee?" he asked as he crossed to the sideboard.

Smirking, Keith waved at the whiskey decanter and offered, "Or something stronger?"

As much as Patrick would love a stiff drink and to forget everything that had happened in the last fifteen minutes, he opted for the coffee.

"Richard?" Keith asked while pulling out mugs.

"Yeah. Thanks," Richard replied before turning his attention back to Patrick. "So? Who's doing this?"

"My guess is Walter," Patrick told the other man. "He was waiting for me when I left the office Friday night and demanded I cancel my date with Brand and go with him." Rubbing his shoulder at the memory of the light bruising hidden under his clothes, Patrick added, "He didn't take too kindly to the fact that I called the detective on him and threatened him with a restraining order."

As Patrick had spoken, Richard's face darkened to a reddish hue, then drained of color. "You think Walter is behind this?" He shook his head. "You said he was an ass on the date, but since you hadn't mentioned him again, I thought that was it."

Patrick sighed as he accepted the coffee that Keith handed him. "Unfortunately, no. I was hoping to deal with it without involving you," he admitted before blowing on the steaming liquid.

"Why?"

"You're his friend," Patrick pointed out.

"Well if he's screwing with your business, then he's screwing with my business," Richard pointed out. "That means he just lost his friend status."

Patrick felt his brows shoot up. "Really?" He hadn't realized the senior partner felt that way.

"Of course. You bring in plenty of new clients, and you're damn good at what you do." Richard cleared his throat, probably trying to control the slight pinking of his cheeks. "So this detective that's coming. He's already aware that you're being harassed?"

Nodding, Patrick began explaining everything that had happened in the last week.

CHAPTER TWELVE

Brand strode into the office building, glancing around the foyer. Spotting the board that listed what companies owned which offices, he searched for Patrick's name. He spotted the firm's name, noting it was located on the third floor, then headed to the elevator.

When Brand hit the *call* button, the doors to his left whooshed open. He stepped inside and hit the *three* button. As he'd been doing since Vance had tracked him down, Brand wondered what the hell was going on.

All Vance had told him was that there was trouble at Patrick's office and it involved him.

Hoping Patrick wasn't injured or being persecuted because he was in a relationship with another man, Brand prepared himself to stand beside his man.

My man. Hell yeah, I like that.

Patrick was Brand's, and he planned for everyone to know about it. While Brand knew his quick turnaround confused his sweet man, that was okay. Brand had pulled his head out of his ass and knew what he wanted.

When the elevator doors opened, Brand stepped out and found himself in a reception room. He crossed to the young woman sitting behind the desk. "Morning, Christy. My name is Brand Erdogan," Brand greeted after glancing at the nameplate. "I'm looking for Patrick. I was told he'd be expecting me."

"Yes, sir," Christy replied. "Just a moment." She picked up her phone and pressed a couple of buttons. "Hello, Mister

Ryzor. A Mister Brand Erdogan is here for Mister Dolcet." After a few seconds, Christy added, "Of course, sir. I'll send him back."

Christy hung up the phone and rose to her feet. After rounding the desk, she beckoned as she crossed to the hall. When Brand closed the distance between them, Christy's eyes widened as her gaze lifted higher and higher.

When Brand's six-foot-five frame towered over her slender, five-foot-eight form — Brand figured she'd be about five-foot-six without the heels — Christy offered him a bright smile. Her eyes gleamed with appreciation as she gave him a not-so-subtle once-over. She even peered at him from beneath her lashes.

"They're in Mister Freedman's office," Christy told him, her tone taking a bit of a husky note. Resting her right hand on Brand's bicep, she squeezed lightly as she lifted her other hand and pointed down the hall. "Turn left at the end of the hall and follow it all the way to the corner office. You'll see his name placard to the left of his door."

"Thank you," Brand replied, easing from her hold. As he started down the hall, he bit back his scoff.

Totally barking up the wrong tree, lady.

Brand's long legs swiftly ate up the distance. He needed to know what the hell was going on. As he'd been directed, he turned left and spotted a pair of double doors as well as the name card heralding it as Freedman's office.

So why did someone named Mister Ryzor answer the phone?

Needing answers, Brand knocked on the door. It was immediately opened by a dark-haired man who seemed surprised that he had to look up to Brand. Seeing as the suited man before him stood only a couple of inches shorter than himself, Brand figured it didn't happen too often to the guy.

"Are you Brand?" the man asked.

Brand nodded. "I am. Christy said to come here to see Patrick."

"I'm Keith Ryzor," the man said, introducing himself. "Please come in."

As Keith spoke, he took a step backward.

Obeying, Brand entered the room. He paused a few steps inside, surprise filling him. There was another suited stranger in the room — Freedman, maybe. Brand already knew the other three people.

Not only was Patrick seated in one of four chairs clustered around the coffee table, but so were his friends, the detectives Carl Lewis and Ryan Straton.

"Hey, guys," Brand greeted softly as he crossed the room. "Heard there was trouble." Part of him registered the click of the door closing, but he ignored that in favor of getting to his lover. Without thought, Brand threaded his fingers through Patrick's hair and used the hold to tip his man's head back. He bent at the waist and placed a light kiss to Patrick's lips. "You okay, honey?"

Brand's worry spiked when Patrick shook his head. "Not really." His cheeks darkened, and it wasn't from arousal. "First, I'm so sorry. I didn't mean to drag you into this."

Forcing a smile he didn't really feel, Brand slid his hand down Patrick's head until he cradled his neck. He gave it a reassuring squeeze even though he didn't have a clue what was going on. His instinctual need to help his lover screamed through him.

"Drag me into what?" Brand asked gently. Spotting the sofa on the other side of the coffee table — a dark-leather piece that matched the four chairs — he slid his hand to Patrick's upper arm. "Come on."

To Brand's pleasure, Patrick followed his urging. His lover stood, and Brand guided him around the table. As he settled on one side of the sofa, he tugged Patrick down beside him.

"So." Brand noticed the white pages stacked on the table as he wrapped his arm around Patrick's shoulders, then shifted his gaze to Ryan and Carl. "What's going on?"

"You're aware that Brand has a stalker?" Carl began.

Brand nodded. "An asshole named Walter."

Carl smirked. "Right. Keep in mind that we don't yet have proof that he did this, but he is our prime suspect."

"Suspect for what?" Brand growled low in his throat as he tightened his arm around Patrick. "Did you get hurt this morning?"

"No," Patrick murmured. "I—" Huffing a sigh, he stated, "You remember what we did Friday night?"

Brand felt his chest warm, but he breathed deeply and kept it from climbing his neck. He couldn't help the way his gut clenched or how his blood heated. Thinking of all the wonderful things he had done and still wanted to do to his lover always had that effect on Brand.

I hope it always will, too.

"Of course," Brand rumbled, holding Patrick's gaze and doing his best to ignore the others. "Why?"

Patrick's cheeks were a dark ruddy color, and he swallowed hard enough that his Adam's apple bobbed. "Someone saw. Took pictures of us. Sent them to my clients."

Brand rolled that information around in his brain. Someone had seen him fuck Patrick? How was that possible? Why take pictures?

"Fuck," Brand said on a growl. "Someone sent pictures of us having sex to your clients?"

As Patrick nodded, he reached forward and grabbed the stack of papers from the coffee table. When he flipped them over and handed them to Brand, Brand got an eyeful. He glanced around, glaring at the others, pleased to see that the other men were studiously looking elsewhere.

"They've seen them, Brand," Patrick murmured, rubbing his palms over his thighs. "Loads of people have seen them."

Brand understood that, but that didn't change his base instinct to snarl at the others. Slowly, he flipped through the photos. He noticed the majority of them were centered on Patrick's body. Brand was more an afterthought, and his face was only featured in the ones where they'd been kissing.

Evidently, whoever had taken them wanted to see Patrick in passion but wasn't interested in anyone else.

"We look hot together," Brand commented absently. He paused at a photo of Patrick tied up, his knees lifted and spread, and with Brand's fingers in his ass. "Love this look on your face, honey." Upon hearing Patrick's shocked gasp, Brand turned his attention to his lover. He saw the disbelief on the man's face, so he grinned and winked. "Might have to keep a few of these. Just cut off the part where he wrote on them."

"Y-You . . . you . . . you're not serious," Patrick declared.

"I am," Brand countered. Knowing it wasn't a conversation for an audience, even if his dick was hard and aching behind his fly just from enjoying the sight of Patrick's gorgeous body, Brand returned the pictures to the coffee table, face down. "So then." Brand cracked his knuckles as he scowled at the detectives. "Where is the asshole? I want ten minutes alone with him."

Ryan chuckled darkly. "Not gonna ask what you want to say to him." The dark-haired detective smirked. "Wouldn't want to have to arrest you."

Brand snorted and rolled his eyes.

Yeah. That would suck.

"And we're not sure, yet," Carl picked up the commentary. "I sent uniforms to Walter's hotel room, but he's already checked out. His ticket to return home was supposed to be Wednesday evening, but it was canceled, so we know he's still here somewhere."

Oh, good. I may be able to find him first, after all.

"Whatever you're thinking, knock it off," Ryan ordered dryly. "We will find him and question him." He turned his attention to the suited man Brand hadn't yet been introduced to. "Mister Freedman, Walter was in town visiting you, right?"

Mister Freedman shook his head. "Not exactly. Walter came to town for a convention last weekend, and since he'd never been here before, he took some time off and asked me to show him the sights." Freedman rubbed the back of his neck, appearing a bit uncomfortable as he glanced at Patrick, then focused on Brand. "I didn't know Patrick was dating someone when I convinced him to go to dinner with Walter."

Brand shrugged. "We weren't dating then. We met the next day." Leaning over, he pressed a kiss to Patrick's temple. "Instant connection."

"Know how that feels," Ryan claimed with a grin. "So, you have two options. Lay low while we track him down, or go out in the open to try to lure him out."

"We'll go out," Brand replied.

"We will?" Patrick stared at him, his gray eyes wide behind his black frames.

Brand nodded. "I'm not an exceptionally patient man, honey." He figured his smile appeared a little feral. "And what better way to draw out an obsessive asshole than showing that we don't care about his antics." Then he leaned over and pressed a kiss to Patrick's temple. "Besides, I haven't had the chance to take you out on a real date, yet."

"I've enjoyed the dates we've had," Patrick whispered, his cheeks turning a much more pleasing shade of pink.

"Me, too." Brand used his free hand to cup Patrick's jaw. Leaning down, he sealed his mouth over his lover's. He slid his tongue out, pressing it between Patrick's lips, and delved deep into his man.

Patrick tasted of coffee, a hint of creamer, and something that was all his man's own.

Brand loved it and continued to lap at Patrick's tongue for more.

"Okay, okay," someone called. "The only person who gets to make out in my office is me!"

Freedman then.

Deciding that making out with his lover at Patrick's work probably wasn't his best decision, Brand eased the kiss to an end. He gave Freedman a wide smile. "Sorry, bud." He slid an appreciative look over Patrick before returning his focus back to the blond lawyer. "Can you blame me?"

To Brand's relief, Freedman snorted as the corners of his lips twitched. "Not my type, but congrats."

Brand nodded, then returned his focus to the detectives. "Can we nail him for the defamation of Patrick's character?" He moved the hand that had been on Patrick's jaw down to his thigh and rubbed soothingly. "What a man does in his bedroom shouldn't be used as a weapon against his job."

"No, it shouldn't," Carl stated coldly, his eyes narrowing. "And he will pay for his actions."

"Good." Brand left it at that. He didn't know the ins and outs of the law, but he knew Carl and Ryan. If the pair said Walter would pay, then he would. Brand turned his attention to the other men in suits. "How does this affect my man's job?" Something else occurred to him. "And how does he know who Patrick's clients are?"

Brand could tell by Freedman's lifted brows that the guy probably thought he was overstepping his bounds. *I don't give a shit.* Seeing that Keith had a slight smile on his face, Brand focused on him and lifted one brow.

The dark-haired lawyer seemed like a more personable man.

"We're not sure about the client thing. We're going to have to do some in-house research in conjunction with working with the detectives," Keith stated, shaking his head. He scowled as he exchanged a look with Freedman. "And Patrick won't lose his job, if that's what you're asking. Before all this started, Richard and I" —*oh, so that's Freedman's first name*—

"were discussing making Patrick a senior partner, but that'll have to wait." Rubbing the back of his neck, Keith gave Patrick a reassuring smile. "After this is concluded though, we'll discuss particulars with you."

"Holy shit," Patrick hissed, his eyes widening. "Really?"

"You're our best junior partner, Patrick," Richard told him, shoving his hands into his pockets. "You know that and so does everyone else here."

"Wait." Carl lifted his hand, gaining everyone's attention. "Does anyone else know you were discussing making Patrick a senior partner? Would one of the other junior members have wanted to discredit him?" Carl waved his hand toward the flipped photos.

Keith growled. "To the best of my knowledge, no one else should know." He lifted a brow and focused on Richard, who nodded in response to Keith's silent question. "We'll give you a list of everyone, though."

"Excellent," Carl said with a nod.

"What do I do in the meantime?" Patrick asked dolefully. "Some of my clients are willing to walk away from me."

Brand squeezed Patrick's thigh. "That'll just give you and me more time to draw Walter out," he stated firmly.

"With your amazing track record, I'm sure you'll weather the storm just fine," Keith assured him with a smile.

"And with your friends by your side, you'll have many new clients referred your way in no time," Ryan vowed, slapping his leg for emphasis. Then he reached out and used a gloved hand to grab the pictures and slide them into a plastic bag.

Brand lifted a hand. "What are you doing with those?"

"Gonna dust 'em for fingerprints and see whose we find," Ryan told him, not batting an eyelash at Brand's glare, and he even returned Brand's look with one of his own. "We'll probably have better luck with the pictures at Vance's though. At least *he* had the presence of mind to stop touching them after he realized what they were."

Most of the men's faces in the room took on a pinkish hue at the admonishment.

However, Brand groaned for a different reason. "Vance saw these? Shit!" He hated that his best friend had seen his lover naked and in the throes of passion.

He's mine, goddamnit!

CHAPTER THIRTEEN

Patrick wasn't so certain going out to eat was the best thing to draw out Walter. Of course, he knew that hiding in his home or office wouldn't have worked, either. With that thought, coupled with how eager Brand had seemed to take him out, Patrick pushed his second thoughts to the back of his mind.

"Patrick?" Brand called from the front of the house. "Where are ya, hon?"

"Bedroom!" he shouted back.

Patrick had given Brand a key to his small, two-bedroom home when they'd left the office Monday afternoon. His man had spent the evening with him, then returned to the farm to work on Tuesday. After working from home that day, Patrick had convinced Brand to stay in that evening.

Not so, today.

After another day calling clients, apologizing for a psycho's actions, and appreciating the few people who were sticking with him, Patrick would be spending the evening at *Surf and Turf Bar and Grill*. He'd been to the nice steak and seafood restaurant a few times but never on a date.

Client dinners had a different kind of tension to them. Something that Patrick was used to. This time, however, he was going on a date meant to draw out his asshole stalker.

"Hey, honey," Brand crooned as he strode into the bedroom. "God, you are so hot."

As Brand spoke, he crossed the room and wrapped his

arms around Patrick from behind. He rested his palms on Patrick's stomach as he nuzzled against his temple. Scraping his fingernails along the waistband of Patrick's pants, Brand inhaled deeply and moaned.

"Smell so damn good."

Patrick whined as he pressed back into Brand's hold. He would have gripped the man's wrists and pushed his hands lower, but his lover had caught him in the middle of tying his tie. Hearing Brand's rough chuckle, Patrick bet his lover knew exactly what he was thinking.

"Finish tying your tie, honey," Brand ordered as he eased away from him with another kiss to his cheek. "I love watching your nimble fingers do that."

Snorting to hide his groan of dismay, Patrick finally managed to finish his Windsor. He had to adjust it a little more than normal to get it just right, but he managed. Patrick figured he was just a little preoccupied by Brand's comment to tie it smoothly.

"You love it when I loosen it even more," Patrick teased as he tucked his tie into his vest, eyeing Brand through the glass of the mirror. "Go stand over there."

Tipping his white-hat-clad head back, Brand laughed loudly. His white teeth flashed. He continued to chuckle as he squeezed Patrick's butt, then lifted his hands in placation as he took a step backward.

"Can you blame me?" Brand asked, gruff hunger entering his tone. His dark eyes were filled with appreciation as he swept his gaze over Patrick's frame. "You're so fucking fine. Now hurry up."

With those words, Brand left the room.

Patrick shook his head as he crossed to the closet. He grabbed a sports coat and pulled it on. While he wore slacks and a slightly dressed down jacket, he couldn't help but enjoy the view that Brand had made.

His lover was big, brawny, and gorgeous in his form-fitting jeans, flannel shirt, and jean jacket.

Sighing, Patrick knew they were a little like opposites, but he wanted them to work so damn badly.

So far, so good.

Patrick kept telling himself that.

After inhaling deeply, Patrick blew the breath out slowly between pursed lips. He picked up his wallet from his dresser and shoved it into the inside pocket of his vest. Then he headed out to greet his lover.

Spotting Brand leaning against the foyer wall, Patrick admired the view as he strode over to join him. Brand's hands were shoved into his pockets, accentuating his gorgeous front bump. The warm smile on Brand's face when Patrick met his gaze told him that his lover had caught him looking.

Patrick didn't mind in the least.

"You're the gorgeous one," Patrick said by way of greeting. Then he rested his palms on Brand's chest, stood on his toes, and tipped his head up.

Brand didn't disappoint. Growling softly, he gripped Patrick's upper arms. Dipping his head, Brand sealed his lips over Patrick's own and took his mouth in a toe-curling kiss.

After thoroughly mapping Patrick's mouth, Brand lifted his head. He licked his lips, obviously clearing the gleaming lip gloss from his lips. Then he hummed.

"Yum. What flavor today?" Brand tipped his head and seemed to be thinking hard. "Something a little citrusy."

Patrick loved that about his man. Brand never minded that his kisses left flavored gloss on his lips. In fact, he made a production of licking his lips clean and guessing at flavors.

"Strawberry pomegranate," Patrick told him.

Brand hummed. "Pomegranate. Wouldn't have guessed that." After winking, he pecked another kiss to Patrick's lips. "I like." Then he straightened and held out his hand. "You ready to go?"

Nodding, Patrick grabbed his keys from the bowl on the end table near the door. "And I'm even a little hungry."

Laughing, Brand stated, "Good. I'm getting steak and lobster." He rested his hand on the small of Patrick's back as he guided him out the door. "Can't remember the last time I had lobster, but it's a special occasion."

Patrick paused to watch Brand lock the door behind them. "It is?" *Special occasion?* "What's the special occasion?"

Brand slung his arm around Patrick's shoulders and started him moving toward his truck. "This is the first date I've ever been on with a man." He dipped his head and nipped Patrick's ear before adding in a low husky voice, "*And it happens to be with a man I've fallen in love with.*"

Sucking in a harsh gasp, Patrick froze . . . and missed a step. Only Brand's arm around his shoulders kept him from falling. His lover helped him regain his feet, and Patrick turned and gripped the edge of Brand's jacket.

"Did you just say you love me?" The words were out of Patrick's mouth before he could think better of them.

Brand reached beyond Patrick and opened up the passenger side door. Then he used his big body to back Patrick up and wedge him into the space. Gripping Patrick's nape, Brand urged him to tip his head back.

Peering up at Brand, Patrick stared into his big lover's deep brown eyes, seeing the seriousness within their depths.

"Yes, I said that I love you." Brand gently massaged Patrick's nape. "Is it too soon to say that?" His eyebrows creased as his jaw tightened. "Probably, huh? We haven't even known each other for two weeks, but . . ." Brand's words trailed off, and he shook his head.

"Definitely fast," Patrick confirmed, his voice equally soft. Sliding his hands up to Brand's face, he gently teased at his man's lips. "But that doesn't change the fact that sometimes, that's the way it happens." With his heart thudding wildly in his chest, Patrick admitted, "My mom knew instantly when she started dating my dad. I think I knew with you, too. That's why the idea of you not wanting more than friendship scared me so much."

"Absolutely want more than friendship," Brand whispered, dipping his head.

Before Brand's lips sealed over Patrick's, Patrick murmured, "Good. 'Cause I love you, too."

Brand growled out the word *perfect* before sealing his lips over Patrick's. The kiss was deep and forceful. His tongue lapping and sliding, dominating Patrick's mouth.

Patrick clung to Brand, a tremble working through him. His blood fired through his veins, and his cock swelled. He moaned into Brand's mouth and pressed against him.

By the time Brand brought the kiss to an end, Patrick's lungs were screaming. He gasped, sucking in a much-needed breath. Peering up at him, Patrick enjoyed his lover's kiss-swollen lips that gleamed with his lip gloss.

"You look good in strawberry pomegranate."

Brand barked a laugh and waggled his brows. "Damn sexy, right?"

"Yep."

Grinning broadly, Brand slowly eased his hold. He peered down at Patrick's groin, then let out a groan. "God, I wanna take you back in the house and fuck you so damn bad, but we have reservations." Wincing, Brand muttered, "The plan to draw out Walter, remember? And our date."

Patrick blew out a breath as he nodded. "Well, that was a good way to kill the moment," he muttered as he felt his erection die a swift death. Seeing Brand's lips twist into a grimace, Patrick rubbed his chest. "Sorry. I didn't mean that how it sounded."

Heaving a sigh, Brand nodded. "I get it." His expression shifted to a smile. "I love you. Now let's go get dinner." Brand took a step backward, giving Patrick room to maneuver.

"Love you, too." Patrick grinned again, enjoying the novelty of saying that to his lover. "Let's go."

Then Patrick turned around and climbed into Brand's truck. He felt the big man's hand slide over his ass, and he chuckled as he settled in the seat. Meeting Brand's gaze, he saw the unrepentant expression on his face before he closed the door.

Twenty minutes later, Brand parked the truck in the restaurant's lot. Patrick exited the vehicle and fell into step beside his lover. When Brand took his hand, Patrick smiled to himself.

While Patrick had never minded public displays of affection, he hadn't expected it of his big lover. His man kept surprising him, and he appreciated that. Patrick felt a warm tingle slide through him when Brand opened the door for him . . . or maybe that was caused by the heat of his hand because he hadn't released him.

"Good evening, gentlemen," the hostess greeted, a wide smile curving her lips. "Two of you tonight?"

Brand nodded. "I have a reservation under Brand Erdogan."

"Of course, sir." The hostess checked her list, then picked up a couple of menus. Beaming another bright smile their way, she beckoned, "Right this way, please."

The hostess led them between booths and around tables to a slightly secluded nook. There was an antique oil lamp on the table, which was lit with a fake flame. Next to that was a small vase with a red rose inside it.

Although the hostess set the menus before the seats on opposite sides of the table, after Brand had pulled out Patrick's chair and he'd settled on it, Brand took the seat to his immediate right. The hostess quickly moved the menus. Brand removed his jean jacket and laid it across the seat of the chair next to him.

Patrick thought that was a fine idea, and after shrugging out of his jacket, he leaned over and hung it on the back of the vacant chair to his left. More comfortable, he relaxed in his seat and returned his attention to the young woman still hovering beside the table.

"Your server this evening is Landon," the hostess told them, obviously realizing they were once again focused on her. "He should be with you in a moment." After one more winning smile, she returned to the front.

Patrick picked up the menu, and Brand did the same. He startled when he felt his lover slide his hand over where Patrick's rested. Meeting his man's gaze, Patrick turned his hand and twined their fingers.

Brand grinned back at him. "Do you wanna split a bottle of wine?"

"Mmm . . . that sounds enjoyable. What kind were you thinking of?" Patrick asked curiously. He knew Brand was more of a bourbon fan, so he appreciated the offer. "You mentioned getting steak and lobster, so you could go either way. Red or white."

"Don't really care, hon," Brand told him with a wide grin. "I'll drink whatever you suggest."

Patrick laughed softly as he nodded. "Okay." He put down the main menu and picked up the wine and liquor list. "Let's see."

"Good evening, gentlemen. I'm Landon, and I'll be your server this evening," a soft tenor greeted, drawing Patrick's attention from the folder. "Can I start you off with a glass of wine or an appetizer? Would you care to hear tonight's specials?"

Focusing on their waiter, Patrick took in his dark green

eyes, mild acne pockmarks, friendly smile, and plump form. He smiled back at the man, telling him, "Do you have a recommendation on a nice chardonnay?"

Landon appeared pleased to have been asked, and he grinned widely. "Either of these choices are excellent." He pointed to two different wines on the list, one moderately priced and one slightly more expensive.

Patrick chose the more expensive one, then squeezed Brand's hand. "Did you want to order an appetizer?"

Brand nodded. "Absolutely. I checked out their menu with my phone," he claimed with a wink. Then he turned his attention to Landon. "I'd like an order of your bacon stuffed mushrooms, please."

Landon hummed as he jotted it down on his order pad. "Excellent choice. Love those things." After a glance between them, he told them, "I'll get that order started and be back with your wine in just a moment."

"Thank you," Patrick replied while Brand just nodded. After the waiter had left, Patrick squeezed Brand's hand again. "Those mushrooms are a great choice."

Brand grinned. "Good." As he turned his menu to the surf and turf options, he asked, "What are you hungry for?"

"You," Patrick quipped back with a saucy wink.

Laughing roughly, Brand gave him a narrow-eyed stare. "Behave."

Patrick leveled a hungry stare his man's way. "Where's the fun in that?" he asked, but then he did return his focus to his menu.

Landon arrived with their wine a moment later, and Patrick urged Brand to test it. He recognized the label as one he'd had before, so he knew he would enjoy it. After Brand confirmed he liked it, Landon poured them both a glass.

Both men placed their orders, then fell into easy teasing conversation as they waited for their food.

As Patrick had expected, their dinner was delicious. He enjoyed the company even more. When Brand had to remove his hand so he could cut his steak, he slid his booted foot up and down Patrick's calf. The move caused goose bumps to rise on his leg's flesh.

Brand leaned close and offered him a bite of steak from his own fork, which Patrick happily accepted. In return, Patrick offered his lover a forkful of his seafood fettuccine alfredo. Wrapping his lips around the tines of his fork, Brand gave Patrick a feral look that tore a soft moan from him.

"How is it that you make eating so sexy?" Patrick whispered as he reached down and adjusted his half-hard prick.

"Just lucky I guess," Brand teased as he eased a bite of lobster from the shell. "Want a bite?" he asked while dipping it into the melted butter.

Patrick shook his head. "Afraid not." Seeing Brand lift one brow in obvious question, he explained, "I'm actually not a fan of lobster." Patrick pointed at his own food. "Give me shrimp or crab any day."

Brand grinned, then popped his food into his mouth and chewed.

CHAPTER FOURTEEN

Brand didn't know if he felt relieved or disappointed that he didn't spot Walter during his and Patrick's dinner date . . . or on any of their consequent dates over the past week. He'd been looking, too. Patrick had shown him a photo that Richard had forwarded to him.

As much as Brand wanted the problem with Walter solved, he always looked forward to getting back to one of their places, so would have hated the delay dealing with the man would have caused. The sex was always phenomenal. Brand couldn't seem to get enough of sliding into Patrick's ass. The squeeze of his man's chute around his erection felt beyond anything he'd ever experienced, and it just kept getting better.

"Hey, you paying attention, Brand?" Vance called before Brand felt a pen bounce off the side of his face. Laughing, Vance added, "Guess not. Thinking about Patrick?"

Scowling at his buddy, Brand bent down and picked up the pen. He tossed it on the desk between them. "And his stalker, yeah." Brand crossed his arms over his chest as he leaned back in his chair. "The asshole still calls Patrick every day, but according to the cops, he's using burner phones. It's got Patrick pretty rattled."

His lover tried to hide it, but Brand could tell. There was tension in his back, shoulders, and neck that hadn't been there when they'd first met. Plus, every time Brand showed up at his door, Patrick's gray eyes were filled with relief.

"The cops still don't have any leads?"

Brand shook his head. "And Carl and Ryan are pretty annoyed by the lack of progress." They'd been to a barbeque at Carl's place over the past weekend, and the detective had apologized . . . more than once. "Patrick feels like he's being watched."

"Really?" Vance leaned forward, resting his forearms on the desk. "He told you that?"

"Not in so many words," Brand admitted. "But I can tell by the way he looks around the area when I enter his home."

"Invite him to live with you."

Brand's jaw sagged open. "Huh?"

"If Patrick feels unsafe in his home, invite him to stay with you."

Cocking his head, Brand opened his mouth, then closed it again. He knew he felt disappointed every time he had to leave Patrick's bed early so he could get to the farm. On the nights they hadn't spent together, his arms had felt empty.

"Do you think Laramie would have a problem with that?" Brand mused, worried about the dynamics between himself, Patrick, Trace, and Laramie. The pair seemed pretty chill about Trace and Patrick's past.

"Why would they?" Vance asked curiously.

"Because of Trace and Patrick's past," Brand reminded his buddy. Had he forgotten, or was he being obtuse?

Vance laughed. "That was all in the past and before Trace and Laramie met." Lifting a brow, an amused smirk continuing to tilt his lips, Vance asked, "What about you? Do *you* have a problem with it?"

Brand shook his head. "I admit that the first time I heard about it, I felt a little uneasy." Scoffing, he shrugged. "Then those naked pictures of us were given out, and I had to squelch those kinds of emotions damn quick." Having trouble meeting Vance's gaze, Brand told him, "I just keep reminding myself that for some odd reason, he chose me, and he loves me. I'm the one he wants."

"Odd reason?" Vance jumped on that, frowning. "What the hell is that supposed to mean? You're a catch."

Appreciating his best friend's indignant tone, Brand laughed softly. "Thanks, man. I just mean he's highly educated, sophisticated, and polished." He waved one hand toward his own body. "I'm none of those things."

Vance shrugged one shoulder as he pointed out, "You know what they say. Opposites attract." Then his grin turned mischievous. "He loves you, eh?"

"Yes," Brand replied slowly, drawing out the word. "Why?"

"No reason." Vance's hazel eyes twinkled. "Just wondering when you're gonna tie the knot."

Brand snorted as he pinned his buddy with a sly stare. "When is Jimmy moving in with you?"

Vance huffed a sigh and leaned back in his chair. "My court date is Thursday," he told him, a low growl entering his tone. "I've already started collecting boxes, although Jimmy doesn't know it, yet. You available on Saturday to help me lift boxes and shit?"

"Sure." Brand grinned at Vance. "Just gonna move him in without his consent?"

"He's already consented," Vance countered. "He was just worried about the timing. The custody battle and everything." Then Vance's cheeks grew dark, and Brand knew his friend well enough to know it was from irritation and not embarrassment. "Having Darlene lay into me regarding the house ultimatum while he was in the room with me didn't help. I've never hit a woman in my life, but I was sure damn tempted when she called him my little butt-fuck boy and claimed he was only with me for my money."

"Fuck! She didn't!" Even as Brand said the words, he knew it was true. Vance wouldn't make up something like that.

Shaking his head, Brand asked, "What did you do?"

Vance's expression turned feral. "I frog-marched her out of my cabin and slammed the door in her face. She started yelling slurs and threats through the door, and Laramie heard." A wicked grin curved Vance's lips. "The boss-man threatened to call the cops on her, and she left, yelling that I'd be sorry."

"Well, you *are* taking her house." Brand slapped his hand over his mouth as he shook his head. Seeing the way Vance scowled at him, he quickly blurted out, "I can't believe I just said that. And I *know* you're not taking her house, you're just not *paying* for her home anymore."

Brand knew the dynamics of Vance's personal life with his ex-wife, Darlene. The woman had used Vance as her own personal piggy bank for over a decade. She lived in a four-bedroom, three-bath home in the suburbs in the *right* neighborhood. There wouldn't have been anything wrong with that if Darlene had worked to help pay for it, but she didn't. She spent her days being seen at the *right* country clubs and schmoozing with high society.

Everything in Darlene's life was paid for by Vance, while she filled Mark's head with slurs and nasty opinions against homosexuality.

Brand had been urging Vance to cut her off for years. When his friend had met Jimmy and fallen in love with the handsome bartender, it had been the catalyst for him to make some hard changes. Fortunately, Mark had been smitten by Carl Lewis's adult daughter, Lorna, and she'd been instrumental in correcting Mark's way of thinking.

"Well, I'll be there to support you," Brand told him, leaning forward again. "You and Patrick. It's the first time he's to go before a judge since the photo incident."

Vance nodded. "Thanks. I hope everything goes smoothly."

"I'm certain it will." Brand chuckled as he added, "Especially since Mark is old enough to express his own opinion about where he wants to live."

Brand's phone rang, drawing his attention. He pulled it out, and his brows lifted. "Huh. Why would Keith be calling me?"

"Better answer and find out," Vance advised the obvious.

Snorting, Brand grinned at his friend. He accepted the call and lifted his phone to his ear. "Hello?"

"Is this Brand?"

"It is," Brand replied. "Keith?"

"Yeah, Patrick is on the phone with the cops, but I thought you'd want to know. Someone started Patrick's house on fire."

Brand leaped to his feet. "What?" He saw Vance also rise, but he didn't bother answering his friend's question. Instead, Brand rounded his chair and hurried toward the door.

"Where is he?"

"He's here in the office, white as a sheet," Keith told him. "He wants to go home to see the damage, but he's in no condition to drive. I'm gonna take him, and I thought you might want to meet us there."

Brand was already halfway to his truck. "Absolutely. I'll see you both there." He hung up the line and grabbed his truck's door handle.

"Brand!"

Vance's hand clamped onto his wrist, pausing his action of climbing behind the wheel.

"What the hell is going on?"

Meeting Vance's gaze, Brand stated, "Someone set Patrick's house on fire. I need to go."

Nodding, Vance released him. "Let me know how much time you need off."

Appreciating his boss and friend's understanding, Brand

replied, "Thanks. I'll keep you posted."

Vance closed the door of the cab, then took a couple of steps backward. "Drive safe," he yelled over the roar of Brand's engine as he started the truck. "Don't speed."

Brand flipped Vance the bird, then pushed his truck into gear. As he turned his vehicle around, he spotted Laramie jogging toward the cabins. He waved at the man, figuring he might have heard through Trace — his firefighter partner — but he wasn't going to stop to find out.

Focusing on his driving, Brand did a pretty good job of following Vance's suggestion. After all, he knew if he was pulled over for speeding, it would just take him that much longer to get there. With that thought in mind, Brand kept to around five over.

Weaving through streets, Brand kept his eye on the horizon. He spotted the smoke from the fire long before he reached the street. Brand parked as close as he could and hopped out of his truck, slamming the door behind him.

Sweeping his gaze over the area, Brand searched for his lover. He spotted someone else, instead, and a low growl erupted from him. Switching directions, Brand weaved through the crowd of gawking spectators.

I'm coming for you, Walter. Don't turn.

Brand willed the man to stay focused in the direction of the burning building. Taking a chance, he followed Walter's gaze. He gritted his teeth when he saw Patrick standing beside Keith, Carl, and Ryan.

Returning his focus to Walter, Brand picked up his pace. He hated the smirk on the man's face and the crazy glow of fanaticism lighting the asshole's dark eyes. Brand was ten feet from the man when Walter glanced around.

Walter stared at him. Then his eyes widened as recognition lit up his features. Pivoting, he ran, ducking between people.

"Shit!" Brand snarled, surging forward.

Brand dodged between members of the crowd, bellowing

Walter's name. To his pleasure, people parted, their shock evident. He barely spared them a glance as his long-legged gait closed the distance between himself and Walter.

By the time Walter ducked into an alley, Brand was only a few feet behind him. He followed blindly, determined to catch the asshole that was bothering his lover. Pain slammed through his calf, and he shouted in agony while stumbling into the wall.

A snarl erupted from Brand when he saw Walter holding the steel pipe and preparing to swing again. He bet the guy had been going for his knee but had misjudged due to their height differences. His next shot probably wouldn't be so off.

Brand didn't give Walter a chance.

Diving forward, Brand slammed his big body into the other man's. He felt the pipe bounce off his shoulder, but he ignored it. His momentum sent them both crashing to the ground, gravel scraping across Brand's knuckles since his hands were under Walter.

Rising to one knee, Brand grabbed Walter's wrist in a tight hold. "Drop it," he ordered, squeezing . . . hard. Brand wrapped his other hand around his shoulder blade — right where Walter had left marks on Patrick — and dug his big fingers into him.

"Let go of me, man!" Walter screamed, writhing beneath him as he attempted to twist away. "Leggo!"

"Not a chance, Walter." Brand slammed Walter's hand against the nearby metal garbage bin. "You're comin' with me."

"No way, I—"

"Brand is right," a deep voice Brand recognized came from behind him. Brand didn't know where Detective Ryan Straton had come from, but he was pretty damn happy to hear the man's gun cock before adding, "You're coming with us, Walter. Drop the weapon."

Walter's nostrils flared, and his eyes narrowed. He looked ready to defy the detective, but then he dropped the pipe. "This is ridiculous," Walter claimed angrily. "I'm an innocent bystander accosted by this ruffian." He tried to sound haughty as Brand released him and rolled to his feet, Ryan moved in to flip Walter to his back and cuff him, ruining the effect. "You should be arresting him," Walter continued to insist. "I've done nothing wrong."

"We both know that's not true, but you'll have your chance to string along some more lies," Ryan told him mildly. Then the detective read Walter his rights.

When Brand began to put his weight on his right leg, pain lanced through his calf. Hissing, he rested his hand on the nearby wall for support. Leaning down, Brand rubbed over his calf. Upon feeling a swollen lump already forming, he groaned softly.

"You all right?" Ryan asked.

"The asshole swung the pipe at me and nailed my calf," Brand admitted as he started limping carefully. "I'll be fine."

"We have an ambulance nearby," Ryan told him. "I'll call them over if you want to sit a minute." He pointed at a nearby lawn chair.

Brand shook his head. "Naw. I wanna get to Patrick. See how he's doing."

"Patrick is mine!" Walter screamed, suddenly sounding deranged. "Mine! Do you hear me?"

Curling his lip, Brand sneered at Walter. "Not in this lifetime." Then, ignoring the pain and the asshole's cries, Brand headed in the direction he'd last seen Patrick.

CHAPTER FIFTEEN

Upon hearing Brand call his name, Patrick turned . . . and his jaw sagged open. Not only was Brand limping toward him, but Ryan followed with a cuffed Walter. He did his best to ignore the asshole's continued assertions of what he was going to do to him in favor of hurrying to Brand's side.

"Are you okay?" Patrick rested his hands on Brand's chest and rubbed even as he swept his gaze over his body, focusing on his leg. "Where's it hurt?" Then Patrick spotted his lover's bloody knuckles. "Oh, Brand!"

Patrick touched his man's wrists, worry filling him.

"I'll be fine," Brand assured, resting his hands on Patrick's shoulders. "I want to know how *you* are." Lifting one hand, Brand lightly pushed Patrick's hair away from his face. "How are you holding up?"

As much as Patrick wanted to sink into Brand's embrace, he needed to make certain his lover was okay first. He also needed to know what had happened.

"I'll be fine. It's just a house," Patrick told him, realizing the truth of his words. "It can all be replaced." Gripping one of Brand's wrists again, he used his fingertips to tease close to the torn flesh. "Tell me what happened, please, Brand."

"I had to park quite a ways away," Brand told him, then explained how he'd spotted Walter lurking in the crowd, most likely surveying his handiwork. "He took off when he spotted me, but I caught up with him in the alley. He got off a lucky shot and slammed a metal pipe into my calf." Brand grinned, feral pleasure filling his tone. "But I took him down."

"And Ryan?" Patrick asked, glancing around.

Upon spotting an empty-handed Ryan striding toward him with Randy and Wade, the paramedic team assigned to the scene, unease trickled down Patrick's spine. "What happened to Walter?"

Please tell me he wasn't released.

"Got tired of listening to his bullshit, so I stuck him in the back of a squad car." Ryan rolled his eyes as he sneered. "The crazy guy can cool his heels while the paramedics check out Brand's injuries. We'll document the attack and add it to the list of charges against the man." Smiling widely, Ryan added, "I'll also serve him the restraining order against you."

While Randy and Wade urged Brand onto a collapsible stool they'd brought with them, Ryan explained how he'd seen the pair running between people, so he'd given chase.

"So, now what?" Patrick peered over his shoulder at the group of firefighters working hard to control the blaze. "Will there be any proof that he burned down my house?" While his home had been small, it had been his place of peace for years.

"I sure hope so," Carl stated, joining the group. His brows lifted when his focus landed on the massive welt on Brand's leg. "Damn, man. That looks like it hurts."

"It does," Brand responded dryly. "I'll heal, though. Nothin' broken."

Wade nodded from where he was busy cleaning and applying butterfly bandages to Brand's messy knuckles. Randy was doing the same to Brand's other hand. "You're lucky Walter didn't swing two inches higher," Wade told them. "He could very well have shattered your knee."

Brand grunted. "Yeah."

"As it stands, you'll have a bruise for a few weeks," Wade continued. "It's deep enough to have hit the muscle."

"Had that happen before, too," Brand claimed with a snort. "Ornery sow got me good when I was in the way to her feed."

Waggling his brows, Brand added, "Her bacon tasted *extra* good."

Patrick barked a laugh. With that simple statement, his lover soothed him. The fear upon spotting Walter—even cuffed—disappeared. His shock at hearing that his home was a complete loss faded. Even the underlying sense of unease that he'd been living with for the last week leeched from his body.

While Patrick suddenly felt tired, he felt jubilant, too. Love for the man who'd stood by his side through it all bubbled through him. Patrick barely resisted the urge to throw himself onto Brand's lap. He didn't think the stool could take it.

Brand must have read something in Patrick's features, for a wide smile curved his lips as he pushed both men away and lurched to his feet. His lover opened his arms, and Patrick pressed against him. Resting his cheek against Brand's expansive torso, ignoring the way his glasses dug into the side of his face, Patrick relished the feeling of Brand's heavily muscled arms wrapped around him and holding him in a firm, gentle embrace.

"Are you okay, hon?" Brand whispered into Patrick's ear.

"I'm more than okay," Patrick replied. When he felt Brand's big hand on his jaw, he followed his lover's urging and tipped his head back. Seeing the concern and question in Brand's dark eyes, Patrick grinned. "Really. I'm good." Glancing toward where he assumed the detective had taken his stalker, Patrick shrugged. "I'm better than good."

"*Good*," Brand responded, urging Patrick to turn his attention back to him. "Now, give me a kiss, and I'll take you home."

"Home?" Patrick murmured, feeling suddenly breathless. He began to peer over his shoulder at the still-burning building, but Brand's hand on his jaw wouldn't let him. Offering his lover a confused look, Patrick whispered, "Home, Brand?"

Brand's wide smile flooded Patrick with warmth, while his next words sent tingles down his spine. "Yeah. Our home. Together. The farm." Tightening the arm he had around Patrick's waist, Brand stated, "I want your home to be with me, your shit spread over the coffee table, your fabulous cooking filling the cabin with fragrant aromas, and your body right beside my own in my bed." Brand cleared his throat, then added, "*Our* bed."

Patrick's heart hammered in his chest as his pulse spiked in his veins. He swept his gaze over Brand's face once, twice, before feeling compelled to ask, "Is this because my house burned down?"

"Yes and no."

Right then, Patrick loved and hated the fact that Brand always told him the truth . . . even when it was difficult. He lifted a brow, hoping his lover would explain.

"Yes, I want you to come live with me, but no, not just because your house burned down." Brand chuckled, his dark eyes twinkling. "I don't want you to have to go through the agony of trying to find a new home. Not when I was already thinking about asking you to move in with me."

"We've known each other less than a month," Patrick pointed out. Sometimes, he thought Brand was nuts.

Brand laughed as he shrugged. "So the fuck what? I love you. You love me. We get on great." Dipping his head, Brand nuzzled Patrick's temple. "Our friends are happy for us, so why do we need to worry about strangers thinking we're moving too fast? I don't care what they think."

Patrick stared deep into Brand's brown eyes and saw the truth there. The man wanted him . . . immediately. The short time of their acquaintance didn't matter to his big lover.

So it won't matter to me.

"Yes."

Patrick spotted how Brand's eyes widened. Then they narrowed, and he growled before dipping his head. As Patrick had expected, right there in the middle of the crowded street, Brand captured his mouth in a deep and thorough tongue-fucking.

Wrapping his arms around Brand's broad shoulders, Patrick ever-so-happily hung on for the ride.

The sound of masculine chuckles filled the air around them as well as a couple of wolf whistles. Brand didn't seem to care. He just kept sliding his tongue along-side Patrick's while breathing noisily through his nose, the sound rattling in Patrick's ear.

Eventually, Patrick couldn't keep up. He needed air, or he was going to pass out. Turning his head, he panted harshly as he rested his forehead on Brand's shoulder.

"If you two are about done," an amused deep voice stated. "I need to speak with Patrick about a few things."

Patrick knew he was blushing, but he couldn't help it. Deciding to ignore it, he lifted his head and turned to find a big older man standing there. The guy had salt and pepper hair, and he wore jeans and a jacket. The jacket sported the local firefighter's station number.

"I'm Chief Douglas Ferrand. I need to speak with you about your home." The fire chief had to stand six-foot-three, and his features were hard and chiseled. The man curved his goateed lips into a smile, but that did little to soften the guy's square features. "I understand there's extenuating circumstances, and I'll talk to the fire marshal about it. Right now, I need to know your routine when you leave. Any idea if you left any appliances on? Heaters? Any electrical issues?" He glanced at his pad of paper before asking, "Where do you keep your flammable liquids? Anything you can think of that might help us pinpoint what might have caused the fire?"

Nodding slowly, Patrick opened his mouth. Then he cocked his head and snuggled harder in Brand's soothing hold. Running through all those questions in his mind, Patrick did his best to answer them.

Unfortunately, it took over an hour before Patrick could get away. By then, he was physically and emotionally exhausted. He couldn't begin to describe his gratefulness when Gary showed up with not only a shopping bag full of comfortable clothes, but also a garment bag which contained a new suit.

"I should have thought of that," Brand grumbled, holding out his hand to Gary. "Thank you for doing this."

Gary took Brand's hand. "It's the least I can do for my bestie." After releasing the man's hand, he waggled his eyebrows mischievously. "Besides, it's your job to care for his emotional state." Gary slid his hand down his torso, accentuating his flamboyant dress—a butter-yellow, form-fitting polo coupled with a pair of light-green, painted on jeans. "My buddy's dress is my domain."

Patrick didn't know whether to laugh or groan. "Please tell me the suite is court-worthy."

Grinning broadly, Gary batted his eyelashes at Patrick. "The suite is court-worthy. You will be the most fabulously dressed man there."

Brand's eyebrows shot up as he stared at Patrick. "Is that good?"

Even to his own ears, Patrick thought his laugh sounded a little uncomfortable. "Not sure."

Gary rolled his blue eyes. "Oh, ye of little faith." Then he sobered. "Did you need a place to crash? You know I have a spare bedroom."

Patrick's pulse spiked upon hearing Brand's growl.

"He's coming home with me." Brand's smile appeared smug. "Forever."

Warmth flooded Patrick as he touched Brand's jaw, sliding his fingertips along his five o'clock shadow. "I like the sound of that, big guy."

"Me, too," Brand rumbled before pressing a light kiss to Patrick's lips. "You ready to get out of here?" he asked, taking the garment bag from Gary.

"More than." Patrick took the shopping bag from his buddy, then drew his friend into a quick hug. "Thank you for this. I really do appreciate it."

Gary's smile turned predatory as he pulled away, and he focused on the fire chief. "Maybe you can repay me by finding out if that tall drink of handsomeness is available?" Gary hummed in obvious appreciation. "You'll be talking to him again at some point, right?"

Patrick peered over his shoulder at where the chief was giving instruction to his firefighters. He found he wasn't surprised by Gary's request. His buddy had always been attracted to older men — silver foxes, he called them.

Spotting Trace and Vincent — Carl's partner — he grinned as he turned back to Gary. "You know what? Even if I don't talk to Douglas again, I can find out his status for you." Then he sobered. "Just remember not to be disappointed if he's married with three kids, and no more trying to convert the straight guy."

Sometimes, if a man ended up straight, Gary could decide he just needed the right man to change his mind.

Gary stuck out his lower lip while shrugging one yellow-clad shoulder negligently. "We'll see."

Knowing that was the best he would get, Patrick gave his buddy one more hug. Then he started along the sidewalk. Brand's limping concerned him, but his big lover waved away his concern.

Upon reaching Brand's truck, Gary waved and kept going, heading toward his *Volkswagen* bug. Patrick smiled as he climbed into the truck. He always did when he saw his friend's vehicle. It was painted a vibrant orange.

By the time they arrived at Brand's home—*my home now, too . . . just wow*—Patrick's energy was flagging. He didn't argue when Brand took his bag from him and told him to open the door. After placing the bags in the bedroom, Brand guided him through the cabin to the back foyer where the laundry room waited.

"Let's get undressed and leave these smoky clothes here. I'll start a load of laundry later," Brand told him before whipping his shirt over his head. He paused as he eyed Patrick's suit. "Or does that need to be dry cleaned?"

Nodding absently, Patrick murmured, "Dry clean only. Sorry."

Brand shrugged. "No worries." He pointed at a rack with hangers. "You wanna hang it up instead then?"

Patrick began to nod, then lifted his arm and sniffed at his suit coat. Curling his lip, he slid it off his shoulders and let it drop to the floor. "Wrinkles are the least of my worries," he stated dryly with a shake of his head. "I'm gonna have to pay a fortune to get the stench out anyway."

Humming softly, Brand nodded as he tossed his t-shirt into the washing machine. "I hope you don't take this the wrong way, because I *sure* love seeing you in your fancy duds"—he winked—"but I'm glad I don't have to wear 'em."

Chuckling, Patrick nodded as he undid his tie and tossed it into the washing machine. "Not offended." He made quick work of the rest of his clothes, leaving them on the floor, as he admitted, "It took some getting used to, but I don't mind them so much anymore." As Patrick waggled his brows, he shoved his underwear off before tossing it in the machine, too. "Although I definitely appreciate the fact that your clothes make it so easy for you to get naked."

Brand waited, nude and half-hard, eyeing Patrick appreciatively. Holding out his hand, he grinned. "Let's go get cleaned up."

More than on board with that, Patrick took his hand and followed Brand through the house. As he looked around the space, he realized he'd never walked nude through anyone else's home before—not even Gary's. Patrick decided the place did indeed feel like home.

Patrick grinned as he followed Brand into the bathroom. While the place was only a one-bedroom, the bathroom was surprisingly large with a jetted tub and a huge shower. Brand had explained that he'd had a small addition put on a few years before which allowed him to renovate the space.

As Brand tugged Patrick into the shower, he sank into his lover's soothing touches. He relished every second of Brand's care. And when Brand opened up his ass and urged him to bend over and place his hands on the shower's bench seat, Patrick happily complied with that, too.

Chapter Sixteen

Brand swelled with pride as he watched Patrick rule the courtroom. With a bearing that showed off his comfort and confidence in his position, his lover explained to the judge how Vance had been bending over backward to support Darlene for over a decade. Then he shared how the woman had not only been doing her best to milk him for every penny she could, but how the money didn't even go to the care and raising of their son.

Patrick even offered several eyewitness reports—Brand's included. These outlined instances of times when Darlene flaunted the best of everything—from shoes to coiffure. At those same times, however, Mark had been in worn clothing and well-used sneakers or hiking boots.

Darlene's lawyer had tried to answer those testimonies with how boys would be boys and wore out their clothes faster than an adult woman would. That might have worked . . . except, Patrick had used his contacts, and through friends who worked in the school system, he countered with statements of when Mark had admitted to getting cleats for baseball at a second-hand store . . . plus other instances of thrift store clothes.

The hardest part of the whole custody battle had been having to listen to Mark talk to the judge. The young man had been encouraged by Patrick and Vance to . . . just tell whatever he felt comfortable with. Patrick had even gone so far as to urge Mark to share what he really wanted, and Patrick would try to make it possible.

Mark had scoffed and said, "No way can you make it possible for Mom and Dad to get along, but maybe a cease-fire from Mom would be nice."

"We can't control other people's actions," Patrick had told Mark with sadness in gray eyes. "We can only control our own."

Brand's heart had gone out to both of them when he'd witnessed that exchange. He figured the whole situation was the hardest on Mark. The young man had believed for years that his father didn't care about what he was up to, and it had probably been a rude awakening over the last few months to discover that his mother was such a liar.

Once the preliminary demands were made and the standard excuses of *this is why Vance is a poor excuse for a father, and I should get my way* from Darlene and her lawyer had been shared, the true mud-slinging began. Darlene and her lawyer started in on the fact that Vance was involved with someone much younger . . . who was a man . . . and who worked at a bar.

Patrick reminded Darlene that Vance being in a committed relationship with a lover — regardless of sex or job — had no impact on Vance's ability to be a good father to his son. He also pointed out that the opportunity to view stable relationships — either his father's or those he worked and lived near — was a good and healthy thing for a young man. Then he quietly shared a folder with the judge describing Darlene's much more promiscuous activities.

Huh. Wonder where he got that.

When Darlene started screaming about faggots and perversity, the judge pounded his gavel and hollered for order. Darlene's lawyer needed to haul her back into her seat by her arm. When she'd glared daggers at him, he leaned over and whispered something to her. At that, her lips curved into a nasty smirk, shown off when she cast a hateful glance Vance's way.

Oh, here it comes.

135

Brand's suspicion was proven true, as in the next instant, Darlene's lawyer rose to his feet. He cleared his throat as he straightened his tie. "Permission to approach the bench." He lifted a file and stated, "I have some information here that speaks directly in regards to Vance's fitness as a father and his representative's appropriateness to represent this case."

"Very well," the judge replied, barely hiding his dwindling patience.

Darlene's lawyer's expression as he approached the bench was one of self-importance, as if he was doing the judge a huge favor. He handed over the file as he cast a scathing look over his shoulder at Vance and Patrick. When the judge cleared his throat, the lawyer returned his focus to him.

"Why are you showing me what appear to be private photos of Patrick Dolcet?" The judge scowled at Darlene's lawyer. Just as quickly as he'd asked the question, he held up his hand. "Never mind. This attempt at defamation is beneath the child court system. Sit back down, Mister Johnston."

"But, your honor," Mister Johnston cried, pointing at the file the judge had set aside. "This proves that Patrick and his association with Vance would have a negative and possibly perverse impact on Mark's young and fragile psyche."

The judge actually scoffed. "Why? Because the man enjoys intercourse?" He shook his head even as he focused on Patrick. "Please be more mindful of where you store your pictures, Mister Dolcet."

"I'm sorry, your honor," Patrick replied. While his cheeks were beginning to glow with a hint of pink, he gamely continued, "I was the target of a stalker recently. That was the man who took those pictures of me and my lover and dispersed them." Tipping his head, Patrick slid a questioning look over Mister Johnston. "I would be interested in learning where Mister Johnston acquired them, seeing as the man who took them has been caught, and his and Mister Weimer's ex-wife's name was not on the list of who he sent the pictures to."

"Indeed?" The judge turned his attention to Mister Johnston. "We shall indeed find that out." Then he pounded his gavel again before stating, "In the meantime, I uphold Mister Weimer's request to adjust custody of Mark, hereby splitting the time between husband and wife by fifty percent. Two weeks with the father followed with two weeks living with the mother."

Even as Mister Johnston opened his mouth to contest the judge's words, the robed man shot a scowl the lawyer's way and held up his hand, stalling the man's action. He continued, "As offered by Mister Weimer, which is more than generous considering the circumstances, either parent is welcome to visit their son while living with the other. However"—he lifted his finger and glanced between the pair—"even though Mister Weimer has offered to continue paying full child support to Miss Darlene, in lieu of the fact that he has been paying for her home for over a decade, as well as the new living arrangement and Mark's age, I am cutting the child support payments needed to be made to Miss Darlene in half."

The judge struck his gavel again, thereby ending the hearing.

"You son-of-a-bitch!" Darlene screamed, jumping from her seat. "You told me this was a slam dunk! You claimed those pictures you bought from Christy, that receptionist hussy, would have Vance's suit thrown out. You—"

"Order!" The gavel boomed. "Order in the court."

Security quickly moved in response to the judge's yelling. They didn't reach Darlene before she managed to slap her lawyer across his face. Then both were forcibly removed from the courtroom.

Brand did his best to keep from laughing.

Well, damn! That explains who Walter wheedled for client information.

Of course the receptionist would have access. Christy sent the mail, after all. She probably knew everything that went on in an office . . . assuming she paid attention.

"Son?"

The judge's call drew many people's attention. It wasn't until most everyone was staring at the man, the commotion from Darlene and her lawyer having subsided, that people realized that it was Mark that the judge addressed.

Mark glanced around nervously. After Vance and Patrick both offered the teenager an encouraging nod, he cleared his throat and addressed the man. "Y-Yes, sir? U-Uh, your honor?"

"If your mother hits you, I can make an addendum."

Upon hearing the judge's blunt words, Mark gaped. His cheeks darkened. "N-No, sir," he quickly replied. "Sh-She never—"

The judge lifted one brow and stared at Mark for a long moment.

Mark scratched his arm, and his cheeks flamed. He swallowed so hard his Adam's apple bobbed. "Really, sir. Your honor. My mom is many things, but she never abused me." Perhaps remembering the testimony against his mother— Brand couldn't imagine how hard it was for him to not only listen to the poor behavior of his mother but also to testify that he wanted to spend more time with his father—Mark flushed deeply. "She was a little caught up in possessions, but I was never hit or cut vocally." His shoulders hunching, the young man mumbled, "That was always reserved for others."

"Very well," the judge responded. "If that changes, that is something that you should share with your father immediately."

Bobbing his head, Mark replied, "Yes, sir." After another second, he added, "Thank you, sir."

Everything wrapped up pretty swiftly after that. The court-room emptied, and Brand crossed to his lover. As much as he wished he could wrap his lover in his arms and kiss the fuck out of him, Brand showed restraint.

Instead, Brand rested his hand on Patrick's shoulder and squeezed ever-so-lightly before pecking his partner's cheek lightly.

God, I have a partner. Fuck yeah!

"Congratulations, honey," Brand offered.

"Thanks, big guy," Patrick murmured with a pleased smile — there might have been a little pride in there, too. "But you and your buddies did all the leg-work."

Grinning and nodding, Brand turned to Vance. "You, too, man. This was a long time in comin'."

Vance smiled — his expression rueful. "True that. Thanks."

Brand reached out and wrapped Mark in a one-armed hug. "I know that couldna been easy, little man, but think of how much fun we'll have now." He figured that wasn't the best incentive, but it was all he could think of.

So I'm not great with kids. Sue me.

Glancing around, Brand fought back a wince.

Damn. Maybe I shouldn't think that in a place like this.

"I have to head back to the office to process Vance's paper-work," Patrick told Brand, resting his hand on his upper arm to draw his attention. "How about I bring Chinese with me when I come home?"

Brand's mouth immediately watered. "Fuck, you know me so well," he mumbled, barely resisting the urge to yank his lover close. Instead, he nodded and grinned broadly. "I'll be waiting."

Even though waiting wasn't Brand's strong suit, he thought he was doing fairly well. The house was clean as were the sheets, and all his laundry was done. He'd also showered and cleaned everywhere . . . literally.

His heart hammered in his chest as he thought about what he was about to offer his lover.

The sound of a car approaching had Brand dashing to the front room. He peered through the curtains. A grin spread across his lips.

He's home.

Instead of greeting Patrick on the porch as Brand normally did, he rushed to the bedroom. He shoved off his sweatpants, then crossed to the nightstand. As much as he wished he could do away with the prophylactics, he grabbed one anyway along with the lube.

Soon. After this step. This step first.

As Brand flopped onto the bed with his supplies in hand, he heard the front door open.

"Brand? Big guy?"

Grinning widely, Brand enjoyed the shudder that worked down his spine. He truly loved it when his lover called him that. *Big guy.* The way Patrick said it made his heart race in a way he'd never felt before.

Brand swallowed hard, then called back, "Bedroom, honey! Set the Chinese on the table, then come here." As amazing as the food smelled, Brand had other plans.

After hearing the rustle of clothing, the crinkle of bags, and the soft thuds of footfalls, Brand realized Patrick was finally making his way toward him. He instinctively squeezed the tube of lubricant, his anticipation ramping up. When his sexy, suit-clad lover appeared in the doorway, Brand's mouth went dry.

Patrick's lips curved into a heated smile. "Well, well, well," he rumbled softly. "What do we have here?"

Meeting his lover's gaze, Brand softly stated, "Several weeks ago, you made me a promise."

"Oh, did I?" Patrick cocked his head as he slowly eased his suit coat off and allowed it to drop to the ground. "What was that?"

Brand's breath caught in his chest as he watched Patrick slowly strip. "God, you're so fucking sexy." He loved his man in a suit and watching him control that courtroom had been such a fucking aphrodisiac.

Patrick grinned as he removed his clothes. "Think so?" His gaze swept over Brand's naked form sprawled on the bed.

"Hell yeah," Brand replied, watching the slow strip-tease. "And that promise . . . you promised to play with my prostate until I screamed."

Patrick froze in his ministrations, his chest bare and his slacks open and his dick on display. "Are you serious?"

Obviously his man had caught on to his intentions.

Brand nodded, leering at his sexy, half-clothed lover. "Oh, yeah. Can't wait to—" He paused. Inhaling deeply, the scent of Chinese food flooded Brand's nostrils. His arousal-flooded brain clicked sluggishly, but an idea to hurry the man up emerged. "Yep. Then after you fuck my brains out, I expect you to feed me that Chinese in bed."

That seemed to get Patrick moving, and a chuckle escaped him. "Wow. Letting me play with you *before* food?" He snickered as he eyed Brand, love gleaming in his eyes. "You really are serious."

Smirking, Brand held up the condom and lube. "To the victor go the spoils."

Patrick moaned and climbed onto the bed. He took the offered items. After sheathing himself, he poured lubricant onto his fingers.

Brand had thought he would think the sensation of having someone play with his ass odd. Instead, Patrick fulfilled every promise he'd made. As his lover teased his sensitive inner muscles and played with his prostate, he writhed, groaned, moaned, and hissed. Brand screamed, begging for more, and Patrick gave it to him.

Enjoying every exquisite second of Patrick's love-making,

Brand knew nothing could top it . . . even the upcoming meal. *My amazing man.*

YOU MAY ALSO ENJOY THE FOLLOWING FROM EXTASY BOOKS INC:

Hacking the Consequences
Charlie Richards

Excerpt

"How's the data mining of Krakow's files going?"

Growling low in his throat, Vincentius admitted, "Not as well as I'd hoped. He either hid his tech-savvy abilities, or he has someone in his employ that is damn good." Turning toward the doors, he fell into step with Aiden as he began walking. "I've been hitting so many dead ends and finding so many false trails, it's ridiculous."

"Damn, I'm sorry to hear that."

Vincentius shrugged. Since all shifter files had to be routed through hidden databases on the darknet to keep them out of the hands of unsuspecting humans, it was no wonder the answers were difficult to find. Those who set up such things were normally fantastic hackers in their own right.

"I just need to figure out who in Krakow's employ is doing this, then figure out their signature. Every hacker has one." Seeing the uncomprehending look on Aiden's face even as he nodded, Vincentius bit back a chuckle. He could get a little carried away talking about his passion. "I'll keep working on it. At least with Councilman Alvaro here, I have access to every single report the Stone Ridge wolves sent us. I can use them to work backward."

"Awesome. Glad to hear it." Aiden gripped his shoulder, the blond deer shifter smiling at him. "I heard Councilman Alvaro is big into poker. He and his wife are putting together a meet and greet poker night on Saturday. Are you going?"

Vincentius nodded. "I am." He'd never played poker with any of the councilmen. In fact, he couldn't recall doing anything recreational with them. "It should be . . . interesting."

Told ya Shane would shake up our boring asses.

He mentally laughed at himself.

Aiden chuckled quietly. "Yeah. That's a good way to put it." Coming to a T-junction, the other man waved and turned toward the left. "See you later."

Vincentius waved and headed toward the right, toward the parking garage and home. He was flanked by the council enforcer assigned to him while within the council building's walls. Each councilman had one, and normally they were considered a friend. His was Tideus Solverman, a big saltwater crocodile shifter. His personal guard and best friend — Seever Kerns, a fellow lion shifter who he'd grown up with, also handled Vincentius's home security. Hell, the man practically ran his household. Seever had fallen into step, flanking him, after leaving the central chamber.

After Vincentius glanced over his shoulder at each man, he asked, "What about you guys? You poker players? You wanna go?" He recalled Seever playing a hand or two, but it'd always been Vincentius's idea. Tideus had been assigned to his detail only two years before, and he still didn't know much about the thick-bodied, powerful male. If neither man wanted the interaction, Vincentius knew he could count on them to find someone who would want to go while still being able to do their jobs.

"If you're offering, I'm going," Tideus replied, grinning widely. "I'll show you all how it's done."

Seever scoffed. "You wish. I'll whoop your ass."

Grinning, he felt pleased that he would have men there that he considered friends.

More than ready to go home so he could get to his nap, Vincentius climbed into the back of the SUV, then leaned his bucket seat all the way back, trusting Seever to drive him home.

His phone beeping penetrated Vincentius's dreams. He groaned as he rolled over and grabbed the device. As soon as he managed to crack open an eyelid and read the alert, he jolted to a sitting position.

All vestiges of sleep disappeared as adrenaline flooded his body.

"Holy fucking shit," Vincentius hissed as he shot from the bed. He just remembered to yank on a pair of cut-off sweats before he barreled out of his room naked. While it wouldn't have been the first time, he attempted to curb the habit during daylight hours. Once his genitals were covered, Vincentius stalked through the house, grumbling under his breath. "Who the hell would hack me?"

Vincentius couldn't remember the last time that had happened.

Settling behind his computer, Vincentius watched as lines of code appeared on his screen. He scowled as he read the person's intent.

Damn. The guy ain't subtle. He has all the finesse of a steamroller.

After a moment of watching where the hacker was going and what he was accessing, Vincentius lifted his hands to the keyboard and began carefully doing a back-hack, tracing the unknown user's steps, so he could figure out who it could be and where they were located.

Hours later, Vincentius stared at the screen in shock. The hack had originated near Stone Ridge, Colorado . . . and the user was not listed as a wolf shifter. Could Shane have unknown intentions, after all? Was he planning to harm the Shifter Council and place Alpha Declan McIntire as the king of all shifters, just as Paraben Krakow claimed?

While the idea seemed ludicrous, Vincentius had to find out for certain. He crossed to his office's intercom and hit the button that would open a line to his security office. "Seever?"

"It's Willow, sir." A female voice came through the line. "Master Kerns went off at seven."

Glancing at a nearby monitor, Vincentius winced. It was almost eleven at night. Slept longer than I thought. "Right, well... I need you to track down Investigator Nkosi Akintola. I need him here asap."

Vincentius heard Willow hiss as she inhaled sharply. Still, an instant later, she replied, "Y-Yes, sir. As soon as I track him down, I'll contact you."

"Thank you."

Vincentius released the button and turned back to his screen. Patience wasn't his strong suit, but he knew he had no choice. For this sort of delicate retrieval, he needed the best, and that was Nkosi.

The black mamba shifter would be able to infiltrate Stone Ridge.

ABOUT THE AUTHOR

Charlie started writing fantasy when she was eight, and after stumbling onto her first erotic romance at age nineteen, she realized her true calling. She now focuses on writing gay erotic romance, normally of the paranormal variety, with heroes of all kinds. With the help and support of her husband, Charlie finally fulfilled one of her life-long goals . . . move to acreage with her horses. You can often find her curled up with her laptop and a cup of tea or glass of wine, creating her next adventure. Charlie enjoys exploring the mountains of her new Oregon home on horseback, 4-wheeler, or motorcycle.

She can be reached at ch.richards2010@yahoo.com
Or visit her at www.charlie-richards.com